ORNAMENTAL

ORNAMENTAL

JUAN CÁRDENAS

Translated by Lizzie Davis

COFFEE HOUSE PRESS
Minneapolis
2020

First English-language edition published 2020
Copyright © 2015 by Juan Cárdenas/Editorial Periférica
c/o Indent Literary Agency, www.indentagency.com
Translation © 2020 by Lizzie Davis
Cover art and design by Tree Abraham
Book design by Sarah Miner
Author photograph © Federico Ríos

First published by Editorial Periférica as *Ornamento,* © 2015

Coffee House Press books are available to the trade through our primary distributor, Consortium Book Sales & Distribution, cbsd.com or (800) 283-3572. For personal orders, catalogs, or other information, write to info@coffeehousepress.org.

Coffee House Press is a nonprofit literary publishing house. Support from private foundations, corporate giving programs, government programs, and generous individuals helps make the publication of our books possible. We gratefully acknowledge their support in detail in the back of this book.

Library of Congress Cataloging-in-Publication Data

Names: Cárdenas, Juan Sebastián, 1978– author. | Davis, Lizzie, 1993– translator.
Title: Ornamental / Juan Cárdenas ; translated by Lizzie Davis.
Other titles: Ornamento. English
Description: First English-language edition. | Minneapolis : Coffee House Press, 2020. | "First published by Editorial Periférica as Ornamento, © 2015"—Title page verso.
Identifiers: LCCN 2019028582 (print) | LCCN 2019028583 (ebook) | ISBN 9781566895804 (trade paperback) | ISBN 9781566895880 (ebook)
Classification: LCC PQ8180.413.A72 O7613 2020 (print) | LCC PQ8180.413.A72 (ebook) | DDC 863/.7—dc23
LC record available at https://lccn.loc.gov/2019028582
LC ebook record available at https://lccn.loc.gov/2019028583

PRINTED IN THE UNITED STATES OF AMERICA

27 26 25 24 23 22 21 20   1 2 3 4 5 6 7 8

Every age had its style, is our age alone to be refused a style? By style, people meant ornament. Then I said: Weep not! See, therein lies the greatness of our age, that it is incapable of producing a new ornament. We have outgrown ornament; we have fought our way through to freedom from ornament. See, the time is nigh, fulfillment awaits us. Soon the streets of the city will glisten like white walls. Like Zion, the holy city, the capital of heaven. Then fulfillment will be come.
—ADOLF LOOS, *Ornament and Crime*

In the garden, the trees were upright, rhetorical,
the avenues upright, the ponds rhetorical . . .
rhetorical,
and the owls in rows, upright, rhetorical, rhetorical . . .
—LEÓN DE GREIFF, "Ballad of the Mad Owls"

ORNAMENTAL

GRACE

1

Today they finally brought in the participants: four middle-aged women whose unremarkable medical histories show no record of addiction or criminal activity. The only peculiarity is that they all had children at a fairly young age, but that's not unusual for women from the inferior classes. I called them to my office one by one for a final screening and some blood samples. None of them appeared nervous, with the exception of number 4, who asked too many questions and seemed hesitant to undress. Subsequently they were taken to their rooms for the first oral dose. 1, 2, and 3 fell asleep within twenty minutes of ingestion, so observations have been reduced in those cases to the monitoring of cerebral activity. Number 4, however, has stayed entirely awake and hasn't stopped talking since the drug took effect. I thought it useful to transcribe what she said:

My mom's husband meets us at the door, he pays for the taxi. Their house is huge, two stories with a yard out front. My mom waits for us upstairs. I'm glad you made it, honey, she says when we come through the door to her room. The kid runs to the bed and climbs up to kiss her. My mom is naked on the floral quilt, opposite a fan, reading a magazine by lamplight. She has the curtains closed. She likes to receive us this way so we can admire her. My grandma is so pretty, says the kid, my grandma is like a doll. And it's true, my mom looks like she's just come out of the box. Last year she had laser hair removal, and not a single spare fold of skin is left, she routinely has them trimmed off by a very good surgeon. The problem is, after so many surgeries, god knows why, she's developed a very rare skin allergy and has to be slathered with creams twice a day. Her husband is supposed to handle this, but he does the job reluctantly, nearly gagging the whole time, as if it's some great sacrifice. Apparently he can't stand the ointments—their greasy consistency, the coconut scent they give off. So my mom takes advantage of every one of my visits by making me do the bullshit treatment instead. Who do you think is prettier, she asks, your grandma or your mom? The kid pauses, thinks, shoots me a sly look. I wink to signal that she can respond as we've agreed. My mom's prettier, says the kid, but only because she's your daughter. The grandmother praises the clever remark.

Soon, the kid's absorbed in cartoons while I coat my mother's body with creams. How's the septum, Mom? I ask when I see her wrinkling her nose. Is it healing O.K.? She gropes for it with her thumb and middle finger, and my hair stands on end. It's getting there, she says. My mom had another septoplasty a while ago, and I guess this one scared her. At night she dreams of her nose falling off and the skull underneath showing through. Sometimes it feels funny when I touch it, she says, like someone else's nose. It occurs to me then that my mom's nose belongs to someone else, that it's the nose of a dead person. And just in case, I touch mine discreetly and tell myself: you're right here, calm down.

When we're finished with the damn creams, my mom puts on a floral robe and we all go down to the living room so she can show us the new figurines. This time, there's a group of characters with wigs and livery and embroidered dresses, tiny glass courtesans she buys on the internet. The characters form a circle around a life-sized red crab. The scene is called Voltaire and his friends, my mom says. Who's Voltaire, the kid asks. My mom says he's a French philosopher. The kid wants to know which of the figurines in the circle is this Voltaire guy. Oh, no, my mom says, Voltaire is the crab. The kid's delighted by the little scene and asks if she can open the glass cabinet, touch the figurines. Then my mother grabs her arm hard, digs in with her nails, opens her mouth, and holds up a finger, but she can't say anything, the words won't come out. She wants to, but she can't. And I see the shape of her skull, pronounced around her ears and temples. I'm forced to intervene to free my daughter's arm from her nails. Dammit, don't touch them, I say. The kid lowers her head in a gesture of false submission. My mother lets go of her. I grab her by the chin, and the kid looks at me, her pupils like two fake coins. Do not touch, I say, really raising my eyebrows so she understands I mean it. Respect means looking without touching, says my mother, having finally found the words.

After a while I join my mom's husband in the office at the end of the hallway. Sit down, the old man says from behind his desk. Around him there's a mountain of diplomas in accounting, statistics, and economics from garage universities, a bookcase with books bound in dark-green leather, and a picture of my mom in front of the Twin Towers. And I can't believe this man was my first, my first love, and now when I look at him all I see is a filthy old geezer drenched in cologne, gray hair dyed red like a squirrel's, and those shockingly shiny pretty-boy shoes.

I'm not sure if it's a memory or a senseless, drug-induced invention.

Outside, the dogs bark for no apparent reason. I look out the window just in case, but there's only the familiar nocturnal serenity of the garden, the pine forest, and, farther afield, the electric fence that shields us from the city.

2

The next day I show number 4 the transcription of her mono-
logue, and she identifies the text as a detailed account of what
happened at her mother's house a few weeks ago. Regardless,
the sensation of well-being induced has been satisfactory, visible in both the patients' neural activity and in their survey
responses. All four claim to have experienced a high degree of
sustained pleasure. Number 4's description reads, "An electric purring that arises in the groin and circulates in exquisite
waves through the arms, legs, and neck." Number 4, unlike
the others, is no ignorant woman. She seems to have received
some type of education.

Before the afternoon session, we go for a walk in the garden.
I try to draw something out of her but only learn that she's having financial trouble, that she owes her mother a large sum of
money and needs the stipend we're paying her. But her real concern seems to be her nine-year-old daughter. What I gather from
her talk of finances and the precarity of single motherhood
strikes me as so sordid that I stop asking questions altogether.

Three hours after lunch, the patients are transferred to their
rooms to receive the day's dose. 1, 2, and 3 once again fall
asleep the moment the drug takes effect. 4 falls into a second
discourse:

The peasant is on her knees praying fervently. Adoration of the young shepherdess. Beside her, a courtesan bows in official reverence before the Apparition. The bear will soon eat the Virgin Mary's living image alive, blue mantle and all. It's a spectacled bear, Tremarctos ornatus. At the end of the hall, you hear panting: the nanny and Sextus. It's pitch-black except for the light of the half-open fridge spilling onto the kitchen floor. The fridge's stomach growls. My mom shouts at someone upstairs. Fireflies swarm the patio and the guava tree. I cross myself, afraid they'll find me hiding there, and fiddle with the pom-poms on my socks. All my socks have pastel pom-poms. The cold tile makes me want to urinate.

When I'm finally able to turn away from the little scene, I look out at the patio, where the gelatin sun greens the guava tree. Downstairs, the nanny sings a tender ballad about the famous battle between head and heart.

The dogs are barking again; there must be something agitating them. I look out the window and confirm that everything's in order. The colored lights of the city's tallest buildings shine in the distance, in very poor taste. Here, at least, the thrum of the forest is audible, and the fountain casts its dying splendor through oversized leaves, bringing to mind an enormous set of false teeth.

3

Another walk in the garden with number 4. When I bring up her last bout of prattling, she explains that her mother uses porcelain miniatures to stage "little scenes" in a pair of glass cabinets. What kinds of scenes? I don't know, she says, it depends, could be anything. When I was little, she'd throw a fit if she caught me touching the figurines. I ask if it's some kind of family tradition or a folk custom I'm not familiar with, something like the assembly of nativity scenes. No idea, she says, my mom's been doing it forever, for as long as I remember. And as far as I know, there's no one else in the family doing the same. My curiosity surpasses mere medical interest, she notices at once and goes quiet, the conversation is over.

In the afternoon, when it's time for another dose, 1, 2, and 3 sleep deeply (though they occasionally writhe with pleasure and their brain activity mirrors that observed during intercourse). 4 presents a similar profile, but at no point does she fall asleep, and her discursive output is constant:

When you see me again, I'll be in the same suit. Open the door so the eloquent image appreciates: one hundred eighty-eight typewriters heaped at the back of an empty room, untouched except for the cool, seeping silhouette of the herd, on an empty floor in an empty building, a once gleaming and beautiful rationalist building, built in the image and likeness of once gleaming and beautiful rationalist buildings in rational cities. One hundred eighty-eight typewriters amassed at the back of this irrational city once clacked away on one hundred eighty-eight sheets of Tequendama Group letterhead, a harmonious, rational discourse to be devoutly recited in offices and corridors in the Ministry of Destitution: when you see me again, I'll be in the same suit, and I won't be millions, I'll be the one exception, the broken mold, the inimitable example, and hear me now, paper compatriots: the character most notably absent from all the old farces is the anonymous one, that Nobody with no physical form, no soul or reality, declares Laureano Gaitán-Gaitán, wearing the very same suit and not so much as a miserable mask—Laureano, that fantastical entity now huddled under a box spring, under the body of a poisoned policeman, under all the camouflaged military poems, on a pile of buzzard feathers, to serve as witness in an anecdote invented by jungle radio dispatch, he's already on the phone, on the coco-phone, summoning forth his great vision for the UPN, the OMD, the RRP, the TRS, and other secret acronyms, or seizing the vestments of priestly animals and going by night to pain's door, threatening pain with extortion, or, on another occasion, signing imagined telegrams of dried monkey meat, Laureano declares, which anticipate charges that haven't been made, or, in the end, it's the engineer who whispers in the Cordillera's ear, of the technical and economic functions of the cold, against the administrative management of an ill-fated Minister of Restitution of the Dispossessed, but without a degree in revictimizing expropriation, declares Gaitán, which Gaitán later confirms. But so much time had passed since then that the typewriters had already come to a halt on the brink of rationalism, and miraculously, all those prodigious, lost-era buildings stayed standing, though none of the roughly one thousand rational windows lit up anymore, besides two or three less-rational ones, which, on occasion, did, and that's how someone in a nearby irrational building, let's just say me, was able to assess the broken windowpanes, the old office furniture, the one hundred eighty-eight typewriters clacking away in the yellow light of the ministerial bulbs without the apparent intervention of any incorrupt fingers, which were busy with sensitive secretarial duties and feeding the teeth a nail now and again, each with one of the secret acronyms painted on in green polish.

After today's session, when the participants are back in their rooms and I'm settling in to prepare my notes, I get a call from the clinic. My wife has been admitted with extreme tachycardia, they tell me. It's the second time this month.

4

Luckily, the doctor attending my wife is an old classmate of mine, the discreet type. She must have consumed a great deal of cocaine, the man explains coolly, without a trace of moral condemnation. I think about our superior training, the professionalism instilled in us at school, the same attitude that kept us from forming close ties with our cohort. The only signal of humanity, buried deep within his words, is the faintest suggestion of triumph: he's pleased to have eliminated an old rival. I grant him victory in exchange for discretion. He accepts and, grateful, leads me to my wife's room, even going so far as to take my elbow as we continue down the hallway. My wife has been sedated. That's what my colleague, who's turned out to be a rotten winner, says. She'll wake up soon, he adds before leaving us alone.

I watch my wife sleep. I get bored and can't stop thinking about the things number 4 says when she's on the drug. What about that last discourse? Was it also inspired by her mother's little scenes?

My wife begins to wake up. She smiles. But the smile quickly sours on her mouth. I have to get back to work, she says, take me to the studio.

She puts on a gray dress, which goes very well with her black shoes and matte red purse. She brushes her pitch-black hair, and it shines like a raven's wing. Before long my wife's elegance has resurfaced in spite of our surroundings, which, thanks to her, seem slightly less sordid. The yellow gleam of the municipal lighting and bits of dead night seep in through the window.

We sign some papers, endure a final triumphant look from my colleague, and flee the clinic.

In the car, neither of us says a word. My wife is nervous because her new exhibition will open in a few weeks. She hasn't shown in the city for a few years, and she's under a lot of pressure, which I suppose makes her exempt from advice or disapproval.

Suddenly, she sees a spate of large graffitied walls. What garbage, she says, more to herself than to me, that should all be removed. Frankly, I have no thoughts on the matter, but since she's the authority on all things aesthetic, I can only agree and confirm: they should leave the walls as they were, clean, free of monstrosities. Many of the murals carry political messages, tallies of the dead or disappeared. "Gaitán is Coming," reads one, the colors lurid in the streetlight's yellow glare. I wonder what number 4 is doing now.

5

Upper management pays us a visit. The directors barge into my office, their two rabidly masculine aftershaves vying for control of the closed system. They're twins who've done everything in their power to hide it, with relative success. A very well-groomed bald man accompanies them. He's the architect who designed the building. A few years ago, after seeing the bald man's name assigned to the impressive expansion of a famous museum, the directors contracted him to design our lab. An unusual task, since the modern facilities had to be functionally adapted to the original structure: an old colonial hacienda acquired in an advantageous deal with the historic proprietors, who had fallen on hard times and were willing to sell for pennies.

I'm not the most qualified judge of the bald man's work, but as someone who uses the lab, I can say that I feel comfortable and secure. Our immediate surroundings seem to form a large, friendly casing. The reception, offices, conference room, and living quarters (for the participants) are located in the old hacienda. Here, the bald man has adapted modern furnishings to the formal exactitude, the sobriety of the adobe walls, the straight lines typical of colonial structures, allowing the exterior gardens to be hinted at or wholly integrated into the space via windows of various sizes and angles. Meanwhile, through an ingenious combination of hallways and sliding doors, the hacienda communes seamlessly with the lab premises, the whitewashed walls gradually yielding to a more metallic palette and industrial materials—iron, aluminum, and glass—in addition to a more sculpturesque set of chimneys and storage facilities made of concrete, carbon fiber, and wood. The end result is a kind of great montage that allows one to pass, with the mere opening of a door, from the stately austerity of the big plantation house to an industrial front room that feels something like a gigantic warren.

One of the directors, the self-styled intellectual, discovered a few months ago that the hacienda is mentioned in several passages of a book written by an obscure nineteenth-century costumbrista. Now he wants to dedicate a room to the hacienda's feudal history, with antique furnishings and quotes from the book plated in silver and mounted on the wall. That's why they've summoned the bald man again, though he seems less than enthused by the idea, which he himself makes clear to me when they've left us alone in my office. The most ridiculous nonsense occurs to them, he says softly. The bald man has been buying my wife's pieces for several years; the upcoming exhibition gives him an excuse to linger. I'm anxious to see the new material, says the bald man. Will they be paintings or sculptures? I have no idea, I reply, she hasn't let me set foot in the studio. Without hiding his disappointment—it's clear he was hoping to glean some information of value—the bald man gets up from his seat and holds out his hand. I guess I'll see you there, he says.

6

Medical emergency during today's session. Number 2 had an epileptic fit, despite the fact that in her clinical history, there's no record of any disturbance of this kind. Two nurses had to intervene to subdue the tremors. Later, with the aid of a sedative, sleep was successfully induced. By all indications, this was a side effect of the drug.

I wait nearly three hours for her to wake up, then I enter her room and sit down on the edge of the bed. Lying there with her hands interlaced on her chest, number 2 resembles a corpse. It's the first time I notice her face, marred by who knows how many crude cosmetic procedures: lips like sausages, the nose of a teacup pig, layers of makeup applied as if with a spatula. There's so much movement there, so many undulations, that for a few seconds, in the semidarkness of the room, the borders of her face appear to melt like colored candles. That face: pure excess, a blaze of intentions, spending for spending's sake, rampant adornment. At moments a certain effect of the light bestows a sudden velocity upon the whole, like watching two tropical birds mate in a cage. And yet she herself seems pleased with her appearance, flirting with the personnel (male and female) and acting like she's doing us all a great service by being here. You had a nervous breakdown, I say. Number 2 straightens up and adopts a stilted pose, the weight of her entire body borne on a single elbow. The hospital robe comes all the way up to her throat but does nothing to mask her enormous bust, constricted by the taut fabric. But there's nothing to be too worried about, I conclude. Just get some rest. And I touch her forehead with the palm of my hand, applying gentle pressure until she's lying comfortably on her back. She looks at me, eyes moist behind emerald-green contact lenses. Rest, I repeat. The unnerving green gaze persists. You're very good to us, Doctor, she says. I somehow arrive at a smile.

7

We've made a few adjustments to the formula. No one wants a recreational drug that simply puts you to sleep. The results have been almost instant: today, all four women remained awake and fully conscious, with marked increases in euphoria and lubricity. Number 3 spent a whole hour gleefully shouting obscenities. We're now closing in on what we were after from the start.

A few years ago, a lab employee chanced upon the hallucinatory properties of a flower of the genus Datura, commonly used by rural women in the cordillera to make artisanal soaps. During a stint in the area, he observed that at certain times of year, the washerwomen in those villages entered into a sort of collective ecstasy when they went down to the river to do their work (suggesting that the substance took effect via involuntary cutaneous absorption). The directors and I dispatched a team of research fellows immediately, and they returned to the lab with samples of soaps and the various flowers used in their fabrication. Within a few months, we'd successfully synthesized the active ingredient.

We were shocked when the drug turned out to be almost innocuous for men (by all indications, testosterone neutralizes its effects), such that we're dealing with a drug exclusively for women. Various consultants advised us to discontinue the project because they believed this limitation would be a commercial disadvantage. In the end, after much consideration, we realized the market for the product was potentially massive, especially given the low manufacturing costs: we'd be able to introduce it into various segments of the population, irrespective of social class.

8

Tear down the idols and raise the icons. Tear down the idols and raise the icons. The revenge of the idols. The Great Revenge. The dismemberment of the icons at the hand of the idol incarnate. The collective concealment of idol images. An idol inside an icon inside an idol inside an icon. A six-year-old girl, let's say me, clandestine crosser of off-limits thresholds. Everything crumbling, rifts in the walls, floors swollen from last year's earthquake. Upstairs, next to the misshapen organ, the icons. Creatures of extraordinary fixity. Adult-sized carved slabs, beatitude rotting in wooden expressions, the glassy, lascivious gaze of those disfigured men who come out from under the ruins asking for alms. Take down and take back to replace with another un-idol. The shroud, a fragment of bone, another of wood, a glass eye not to see with. Cancel and conserve with a single spiritual movement, watch as the wooden icon finally appears, the image of Saint Nikephoros, discover with horror that insects have made their home in his thorax. Stay on hoping they'll catch you, but in the end, they don't. Discovery is impossible. Draw back the veil and you risk destroying the face. So tear down the faces and raise the heads. The revenge of the heads. The thousand heads of the cancelled un-icon. An alarm clock man whose job was to wake everyone by knocking his stick against neighbors' windows. The era of dreams interrupted by work, praying to idols for the return of payday. Children playing with shrapnel. A crow with the edge of a sheet in its beak, drawing it over a sleeping boy. The map of London in a woman's glove. Tear down the salaries, raise the idols.

It's nighttime now, the dogs are barking, I look out the window, and down below, at the foot of the yellow stone fountain, is number 4. I decide to go and find her.

To announce myself, I rustle some fallen leaves with each step. Number 4 smiles when she sees me emerge from behind a large ceiba branch. I take her arm as we stroll along; she allows me to escort her through the darkness, beneath the big trees. I ask if she has ever experienced an earthquake. Why do you ask, she says, her brow furrowing. Because of something I heard you say in today's session. I have, she says, just once, when I was a kid, in a little colonial town full of churches that fell down and stayed that way for decades. I grew up there, in a house that looked a lot like this one, she adds, gesturing to the façade of the hacienda. We're quiet for a while, then, perhaps uncomfortable before so much silence, she asks, Do you like colonial churches? To tell you the truth, no, I don't. She looks shocked. But that's impossible, she says, they're so beautiful. I explain that I can't stand the gaud, the molding, that overwrought style, and much less the icons, the saints and archangels. They scare me, I say, mostly because they're not too far off from the kinds of things the narcos were partial to

21

back in the eighties. A delighted cackle escapes her, and I confirm that she's no ingénue: when a woman laughs intelligently, there's a particular kind of music, a crystalline splash of very well-sequenced notes. It's completely different from the sound those decorative women make when they laugh to appease men. If it were up to me, I say, just so she'll keep laughing, if it were up to me, I'd have all the churches torn down, all the saints burned. Her laughter slips nervously through the gaps in the thick disorder of branches. The dogs bark.

9

Anamorphosis, I hear my wife say at a distance.

Maybe the things number 4 says in the trials are a variant of anamorphosis, the art of making an image appear from a nearly unrecognizable angle, a calculated distortion of perspective. What I mean is, what if everything that seems so fantastically deformed in her discourses could be read in its proper proportions with the aid of a device? Like those cylindrical mirrors that, when placed on a table just so, reflect "normal" versions of the flattened, elongated drawings on its surface. It's also very possible that, as happens with anamorphosis, once translated to their normal aspect, the words would say much less than was suggested by their deformed state. What matters with anamorphosis is the distortion itself and not the hidden form. Perhaps, as my wife likes to say, we have to completely renounce our urge to interpret.

We have to completely renounce our urge to interpret, my wife says to a very handsome young bearded man, the reporter who's doing the interview. I'm sitting on the couch across the room, a cup of steaming green tea in hand, following the predictable course of each response as if listening to a stale melody. Outside it's raining; the city panorama streaks the glass. It's crucial that we acknowledge the fragility, the near nonexistence, what we might even call the infra-existence, of materiality (over the course of this sentence, my wife brushes her nose with the back of her hand several times). And I say *materiality* because I want to call into question the very notion of *work* itself. There is no work. There's only the subtlest substance, insufflated with materiality, or rather, with movement, beginning with a primary gesture devoid of any meaning, with one piece sometimes even becoming indistinguishable from the next. The bearded kid makes no effort to hide his admiration for my wife, crossing and uncrossing his legs, smiling with glittering eyes. Give me more, he seems to say. And she complies: When the gesture is naked, divested of any excess of feeling or intentionality, what's left? Well, there's only one name I can think of for that: *grace*. The reporter tries to rise to the occasion, but inside his reporterly head, there's nothing but a heap of sawdust and crumpled newsprint: Yes, your pieces give off the kind of silence that's usually reserved for Eastern art, he says with a satisfied smile, as if he's just let slip his genius. Silence! my wife repeats. Silence, of course! Enough with cheap talk! Because that's what art has become in this country, pure political jabbering, pure opportunism, poverty porn. And in the face of such political hypertrophy, I have to ask: What's to become of profundity, quality, intimacies, not just within the discipline, but within our lives? Circling back to the matter of grace: for me, it's about recovering the mystical significance of the word. By the grace of the Holy Spirit, so to speak. And then, of course, there's the idea of foregrounding the minutiae, the insignificant, the detritus, a practice of gratitude and humility before grace. It's an inaction, really, a non-doing. A twig, some yarn, a scrap of monochrome fabric. The gray! the reporter exclaims. There's so much gray! Yes, my wife says, suddenly lifeless, all libido deflated by his inanity. Yes, there are a lot of gray tones in this last series, she murmurs, and the interview concludes.

She walks the reporter to the door, and I stay near the window, dazed by the rain. My wife comes back and sits next to me on the couch. I'd like to tell you about someone I met at the lab, I say. She looks at me, intrigued.

10

The best kind of makeup is the kind you don't notice, says number 1, a woman practiced in pathological discretion.

Oh, shut up, 2 responds, the whole point of putting on makeup is so people notice.

There's a middle ground, says 3.

Number 4 doesn't offer an opinion because she doesn't wear makeup. Or perhaps she applies it so well it's undetectable.

I just think it's so sleazy to go around with your face painted on, 1 insists.

Don't be such a prude, says 2, everyone looks better with a little color. Makes it easier to play up what you like and hide what you don't.

True, says 3, but go too far with the blush, and you'll end up looking like a clown. Or worse, a drag queen.

Then number 2 turns to me with her finest pout. What do you think, Doctor? Do you prefer us with makeup, or without?

I don't even consider responding to that question. Number 4 can't take it anymore and lets out one of her beautiful, deep laughs (the sound of breaking glass needles the pit of my stomach). The only plausible response is a withering look of reproach that will force number 2 to lower her gaze, something she either won't or doesn't know how to do. Instead, she makes an expression that manages both defiance and playfulness, and I'm lost in the grotesque folds of that poorly reconstructed face, in the layers and layers of makeup collapsing in on themselves as if in a horrendous mise en abyme.

I have nothing against makeup, I finally say, nearly asphyxiated after my time in the cave. None of them seem satisfied with my reply, but at least their attention shifts away from me and back to the TV program. Today is a rest day; there will be no dose.

11

From the domestic worker's radio: a tender ballad about the famous bipartisan conflict between faith and reason. Dr. Paper Heart breaks the shell of his egg, incubated by a black hen for sixty-seven years. He breaks the shell with the umbrella's metal tip. He's born in the same suit as last time, a black three-piece chalk stripe, a black felt, big-city cap, he looks just like a scholar or, worse, like a cop, and against all odds, he begins to complain about the weather: he detests the mountain fog, the fine, filmy rain, the cold that dampens the bones. May this skyscrapered Soria blaze! Music, goddammit! Ayombeee! The Ministry of Tropicalization broadcasts a musicalized bulletin complete with palm trees and coconuts, but it's useless. The theological dispute contracted a virus cured with several apostate decapitations, which the authorities called a settling of scores, the same virus that runs up and down the doctor's voice as, newly emerged from the egg, he cries out to the four winds, in the name of all Spains, for the grammatical enthronement of faceless heads. It's not pronounced that way, not written that way, not thought that way, shut up, the bulletin says. Who needs a brain with an ass like that, baby. Then they passed the law that said black hens could lay their eggs on every corner. The city filled up with doctors. Your signature means nothing, sir, sign here. May it burn! May the animals come down from the mountain and seize the Cholesterol Palace! But it's useless, the tender ballad repeats the doctor's beloved nouns. The domestic worker turns the radio off when there's nothing left to clean. Everything is clean. And someone, let's say me, has wet underthings, has wet herself. We're going to hear that song again. But the faceless domestic worker has nothing left to clean anymore, everything's clean, as clean as can be.

One reason I prefer to stay late at the lab is that by now, the traffic isn't so bad and I can drive home on empty avenues. It's humid tonight. It hasn't stopped raining all week. My feet feel like ice.

In spite of the statistics and the city's undeniable dangers, I've never been the victim of an act of violence. I've never been robbed, never had a gun pointed my way, nothing. Maybe that's why I'm able to drive down these streets without any apprehension. Some drivers speed through red lights, afraid to idle at the corners. Whereas I take a distinctly guilty pleasure in the compaction of these decidedly ugly things, even find a certain beauty there: in the stillness, the tenuous light against the eroded geometry of the façades, the people who dare to walk around here at this hour, hands in pockets and heads bowed. There's an extraordinary fixity in all this. Number 4 said something like that. Romanticism, my wife would say, the consolation of ugly cities.

When I arrive at the apartment, I'm met with a small gathering. The table in the middle of the room is filled with fat lines of cocaine. Music at top volume. Gallerists, critics, artists, museum directors, curators, what my wife would call industry people. The party lasts until four in the morning. I don't think I'll go into the lab tomorrow.

12

Day spent in bed with a colossal hangover, headache, nausea, a desire to die, low self-esteem, disproportionately bad omens. The universe smiles upon you, I repeat to myself, but it's no use, I close my eyes, and my head fills with unsavory images: portent, augury, cockroach, mouse, the directors, Laureano Gaitán-Gaitán, the Cholesterol Palace, a loaded tamal, it falls on me to separate what's edible from bits of shrapnel, nails, bolts, screws, glass, the tamal explodes right at the foot of the statuary, tear down the idols and raise the icons. Wasn't that Hernán Cortés?

My wife got up early and went to the gallery to finish mounting her show. The opening is in two days. I wallow in self-pity and the sticky sheets, sleeping poorly at intervals.

Around noon, I get up, shower, and shave. I google the phrase and confirm that it's Hernán Cortés. I breakfast copiously, and while looking for something to read among my wife's many books, I remember what my father used to say to reproach me for my idleness: you fuel up for the day just to sit back down and do nothing. I've always been a slacker, ever since I was a child, and nothing, not even a strict education, has managed to inspire a shred of guilt in me for it. I'm a deadbeat with impunity. And I'm convinced that, contrary to what my father believed, my lifestyle is very well suited to today's modes of production. Even my hangover could be an oblique form of cooperation with the system: at this very moment, someone's pockets must be filling up at the expense of my malaise, though I couldn't say how, exactly. These days, no one really knows how money is made. My wife says it clearly enough: one must refuse to *do,* must reside in the poetics of inaction. And then millions will rain down upon you.

I try to read a novel and can't get past the first lines. Lying back on the sofa, I fall asleep and dream of the women at the lab, a dream I forget upon waking, as the sun begins to set.

13

PARTICIPANT NO. 1:

Age: 31

Are you a habitual drug user?

☑ YES

☐ NO

What substances do you regularly consume?
Valium, Xanax

How does our drug compare to others?

☐ SUPERIOR

☐ ABOUT THE SAME

☐ INFERIOR

☑ OTHER: *Very superior*

Would you be willing to pay for the repeated use of our product?

☑ YES

☐ NO

Please briefly describe the effects:

Makes me feel looser and more comfortable with others. When I take it, it gives me confidence and like I can focus, I feel I talk better, clearer, people get what I'm saying. And everything looks prettier. Life is more beautiful.

PARTICIPANT NO. 2:

Age: 28

Are you a habitual drug user?

☑ YES

☐ NO

What substances do you regularly consume?
Cocaine, marijuana, heroine, bazuco, speed, ecstasy

How does our drug compare to others?

☐ SUPERIOR

☐ EQUAL

☐ INFERIOR

☐ OTHER:

Would you be willing to pay for the repeated use of our product?

☑ YES

☐ NO

Please briefly describe the effects:
I don't know, juicy, delicious, like you've got wings coming out of you or your hair standing on end. Like an animal in heat or tingling all over.

PARTICIPANT NO. 3:

Age: 34

Are you a habitual drug user?

☐ YES
☑ NO

What substances do you regularly consume?
Rarely I do a line or smoke a joint.

How does our drug compare to others?

☐ SUPERIOR
☑ EQUAL
☐ INFERIOR
☐ OTHER:

Would you be willing to pay for the repeated use of our product?

☐ YES
☑ NO *Would have to be your treat.*

Please briefly describe the effects:
Really cool, it makes you nice and drowsy, makes you want to do private things, you dream colorful little cartoons and pieces pop out in the shape of triangles, circles, spirals. There are visions and nice memories too.

PARTICIPANT NO. 4:

Age: 27

Are you a habitual drug user?
- ☐ YES
- ☑ NO

What substances do you regularly consume?
None. But I've tried some before, the usual ones.

How does our drug compare to others?
- ☑ SUPERIOR
- ☐ EQUAL
- ☐ INFERIOR
- ☐ OTHER:

Would you be willing to pay for the repeated use of our product?
- ☐ YES
- ☐ NO

Please briefly describe the effects:
If you're sad, it makes you happy. If you're too wound up, it calms you down, if you need energy, it gives you some. It's a dangerous drug because it gives you what you need, always, a smart drug that can fill in for anything, meet any desire. It could satisfy anyone. And there are no side effects, not even a headache, there's nothing.

14

Dinner at the directors' place to celebrate the launch of the new product. We're joined at the table by two new investors, both insufferable brats. The conversation is intolerable. I try to resist the puerile exchange, but frivolity is always stronger than temperance, above all if one is attentive to details. Another sad legacy of the narco-baroque period was a propensity for hyperbole, for emphatic gestures, for scoreboards flashing power in neon, with built-in speakers, of course. And the way these people behave puts a twist on that game of ostentations: they conceal the narcos' characteristic bad taste beneath a mantle of minimalism, a fake hide they designed for the old baroque animal, the cathedral's flamboyance stuffed into a cube of monochromatic panels.

The violence in the air is the product of that postbaroque exercise in repression. Here, to the canine nose, a chemical war is unfolding—between aftershave lotions and bodily humors. I wonder, then: Wouldn't that make my own taste a superior form of repression, another layer removed from the one where these four idiots breathe in one another's noxious fumes? A dense atmosphere I can only endure thanks to my thorough training in mechanized smiling and aphorism.

The second cause for celebration is that the managers, availing themselves of their far-reaching paws in congress, have succeeded in toppling a bill that aimed to regulate the sale of hard drugs, a precursor to total legalization. They propose a toast to the well-timed coup. And we toast, of course, because this guarantees us continued dividends from the business and will likely delay the dreaded overhaul that would completely legalize both consumption and trafficking.

I wonder if under such circumstances my job would no longer be considered an aberration. Maybe my wife and I would occupy the same ecological niche, something like "designers of artificial emotional states." Maybe I, in my own right, merit the title of artist just as she does.

One of the directors, the one without intellectual aspirations, wants to tell us the salacious details of their negotiation with the congressmen. His brother leans over to squeeze his elbow and proposes another toast. To the new product, which, by the way, has yet to be christened, he says. Any ideas? The new investors propose names with angelic, celestial echoes (what we repress finds its way out somehow). I detest naming my creatures and so limit myself to applauding each initiative.

15

Today I showed my wife the transcriptions and she remarked offhandedly that they had their grace. I thought it odd that she chose that word, and I told her so, reminding her what she herself said a few days ago about the mysticism of grace, the slender reflection cast back when the affectations of consciousness are shed. My wife said I overestimate language, that I take her digressions too seriously. Especially, she said, since she's indifferent to the meaning of whatever it occurs to her to say. I'm just threading together ideas, like someone adding colored beads to a string, she said, following only an intuitive criteria, like in a child's matching game. That's what grace is, she says. Like the grace of a marionette, which, even lacking will, can move in accordance with the most basic geometry. Meaning is an accident, a surplus. The only thing that really matters is geometry. Circle, square, triangle, line, point. There's no more mystery to it than that.

Fine, I think now, looking out the window as the dogs bark, but the fact remains that number 4 is, in some way, a marionette. Imbued with grace.

There are two participants kissing next to the fountain. Numbers 1 and 2, I think.

16

My naked mother on the quilt, reading a magazine by lamplight. Beautiful as a doll. It's time for the cream, honey, put a little on me, be good. I grab the wrong tube, the one for erasing, I grease my hands with it, and they blur. My mother's eyes are closed, she doesn't realize that I'm erasing her with my hands, my hands pass over the skin of her thighs, and her thighs disappear. Although no, they don't disappear, exactly, they smudge. Now for the hardest part: I'm going to blot out her face. I begin by pressing what's left of my thumbs to her eyebrows, effecting a deep, circular movement that dilates all the way to the edges. After a while, only the mouth is intact, a hole in a stain where the strokes of my fingers are visible. The mouth opens for air; I prefer to leave it untouched. I proceed to blot out the rest of the body. I try to be quick so my mother won't notice. Soon, there's only a large, dull stain on the bed, a half-open mouth, false teeth.

The kid enters the room and sees her grandma has been applied to the quilt, but it doesn't seem to register. The mouth goes on talking: Don't stop, that feels nice, just a little more cream, be a good girl, now. The kid and I laugh softly. My hands have become two smudges, too; it hurts a little, but I can't complain. Don't touch me, just in case, I say. We leave the mouth there talking to itself (oh, that feels good, don't stop . . .) and go visit the figurines. The kid wants to know if she can touch them. Of course, I say, do whatever you want. They're yours now.

At the back of the house, my mother's husband whistles to the song on the domestic worker's radio. That old song about the famous conflict between conscience and reason.

Night falls and I take a walk through the garden. I go beyond the ring of trees that encircles the fountain then follow the black gravel path through a meadow lined with flower beds until I come to the pine forest. It's been weeks since my last visit. It's a very agreeable place, very conducive to resting. The hum of the electric fences towering at the other end of the forest filters through the semidarkness and the heavy scent of sap. I sit, lean against a tree trunk, and think about grace: a basic geometry beyond the affectations of our actions, beyond the will, which lays waste to everything. All the rest is excess, or so my wife says. But what do I think? I've always accepted my wife's most grandiloquent notions as true. But she herself admits that she does no more than join the simplest ideas together, like threading colored beads on a string. She doesn't think like a scientist; she thinks like a theologian. A few months ago we spent some time in the country, on a farm belonging to a colleague of hers. On our daily walks in the woods, she and her friend never tired of rhapsodizing about nature's perfect, ordered world, frankly idiotic comments prescribed by a paltry environmentalism. Then came the day when

I was compelled to explain that the idea of ecosystems as clockwork entities in perfect equilibrium with the cosmos was obsolete, that in the history of the planet, we've suffered ecological catastrophes far worse than the present one, whether provoked by ourselves or simple geological agents like bacteria and wind, and in spite of which life has always managed to prosper. In fact, I say, if it weren't for some of those catastrophes, our species wouldn't exist and neither would the fine arts. My wife and her friend are so outraged that we abandon the subject completely.

I like my wife's work, would even say I genuinely share her intuition about the simple forms, and that's one reason we're living together, but her notion of grace collapses against the reality of the history of this planet as one great and immeasurable catastrophe. The idea that some things are essential and others are excess also collapses. Because nothing is excess, really. There is nothing that's strictly decorative or superfluous. Everything serves a purpose, to the very degree that nothing serves any purpose at all. And in nature, no one knows who they're working for, as the saying goes. I, for instance, have no idea who's running this company. Sometimes I think I'm my own boss. Sometimes I think the directors want me to think I'm my own boss, with my own rules and hours. Sometimes I get the feeling that they don't know anything either. That the job lies in just that: pretending we're each doing our part.

I come to my feet and decide to take a different route back to the lab. One side of the forest rises to meet the main road, where the cars come in. There, beside the enormous entry gate, is the kennel for the dogs, who today are stretched out on the ground and appear very calm. I crouch down to pet them and they growl indecisively, curbing the urge to attack. Gradually, they relax. Not long ago, these two rottweilers were playful pups. Since then they've received special training, and their behavior toward humans is now ambivalent. They've been turned into solitary machines. But something inside them, not wholly repressed, remembers affectionate contact and play.

That's when number 4 appears, as if from the shadows themselves. I straighten abruptly. Pardon me if I scared you, she says and asks for another dose. Her face says she really needs it. I stare back at her, unsure what to do. Finally, I decide to invite her to the opening.

17

While number 4 tries on the dresses I brought in for her this morning, I ask what kind of education she received. She responds from behind a screen that she wasn't able to finish college. I'm in the wooden chair next to the picture window in her room, through which the garden is visible. I had to stop studying when I got pregnant, she says. I was living alone with my mom. My dad had died. My mom kicked me out, and I had to find work right away to support my daughter. So you didn't study at all? No, not really, she says, a couple semesters of law. But you're not an uncultured woman, I say, one notices these things. Then she comes out from behind the screen in one of my wife's favorite dresses, which fits her sound body so well it looks like it could have been made for her. That suits you very nicely, I say. I'll come by for you after the session tonight. Try to be ready. I don't want to be late.

18

My wife tries not to look surprised when we come through the gallery door, but her eyes appear to roll back in her head the moment she recognizes the dress, the fine green fabric accentuating number 4's generous form as she wanders joyfully among the understated pieces. Her presence alone is a gross challenge to the twigs and strips of canvas that dangle as if afloat in the void, the bits of metal skillfully joined to the remains of an overturned chair, the geometric watercolors, pallid and yawning on the walls.

I thought you might enjoy the contrast, I say to my wife. She manufactures a smile. It's certainly quite a surprise, she says and kisses me, trying hard to maintain her excitement. We're interrupted by a band of sycophants come to congratulate her. Are you glad I brought her, I ask when they've left us alone. My wife considers the question, tries to read my intentions, makes a general sketch of the situation. Yes, she says, I'm happy, I can't say I understand it, but I'm happy. Now, if what you wanted to do was make the opening more interesting, you've succeeded, she adds. Number 4's unstudied path through the room has drawn the attention of everyone in it.

I brought something else for you too, I say, placing a dose in her hand. Is it the new one? my wife asks. She gives me a satisfied smile, brings the pill to her mouth, swallows it with a sip of whiskey. I love you, she says. Another kiss and she's off to find number 4. She greets her warmly, takes both her hands, I have no idea what she's saying, much less how number 4 will respond. Then two peals of laughter rise briefly above the din before landing in a ditch with the other broken things.

ECONOMY 1

1

It's not the first time we've introduced a third person into the relationship.

Of course, it's hardly something we can boast of. Group sex became a vulgar habit the moment it gained popularity among white-collar workers. What's fashionable these days is a steady partner, kids, a house in the country, a garden, a folk music collection.

It so happens that last year a young man writing his graduate thesis on my wife's work began to frequent our apartment. A few weeks later, she told me she'd slept with the guy in her studio. I felt nothing resembling jealousy. I understood that my wife actually wanted to be with both of us at the same time, and to appease her, I agreed. It was obvious that this young man was no more than an accessory to our love, a channel through which my wife could transmit the desire she'd honed for me. The young man was a marionette. We maneuvered him as we pleased, leveraging his candor and the admiration my wife roused in him. Week by week we wore down his initial masculine vigor, feminizing him by degrees, reducing his vitality and initiative until he became no more than a plaything. My wife's fantasy of absolute penetration was replaced with the destructive pleasure of watching me come in the young man's mouth. In the end, he agreed to it all without putting up any resistance, his will reduced to the enigma of obedience. Naturally, boredom wasn't far off. The arrangement lasted less than two months, and it was my wife who dispatched him in the end, refusing to see him again even about the thesis. I don't know what became of the poor kid.

Now that the trial is over, number 4 has asked to stay with us for a few days. Her reasons for not going home have been fairly nebulous, but my wife is so smitten with the idea that I'd accept whatever explanation. Number 4 and my wife have very quickly developed a complicity that scares me. I often catch them whispering to each other, exchanging looks I can't decipher. Sometimes I think they're trying to shut me out of the triangle. And worst of all, the link between them intensifies when they're on the drug, to which they are now definitively addicted. So much so that I've been obliged to restrict them to two daily doses. In spite of these practical details, the truth is, I can't complain. I enjoy our time together very much. Number 4 continues to be somewhat evasive in our day-to-day dealings, but she's solicitous when I summon her, even if my wife isn't around. I can sense that she feels indebted to us, and, although I'm certain she gets equal pleasure from being alone with me, I can't help but think the sex is her way of repaying our hospitality.

Oddly, since she left the lab, number 4 has stopped producing discourses on the drug. At most she'll babble if it makes her tired, or she'll converse normally with my wife. Number 4, it turns out, is a stupendous conversationalist. As suspected, she's an educated woman, though she still won't reveal to us when or where she learned so many things. Self-taught, she says. Which no one believes.

2

With the distribution of the new product now underway, the lab has returned to focusing on its legal activities. We've also been contracted to produce generic drugs for the government's mandatory health plan, so the administrators and lawyers who negotiate state bureaucracy are the ones whose noses are now to the grindstone. The machines and facilities, on the other hand, are automated to such a degree that they hardly require personnel to attend to them. The enormous lab corridors are perpetually empty, the only sound the distant hum of factory equipment. I miss the women, the nurses, the staff we subcontracted for the evaluations. This place is too big, we're far too small a number to fill it, and the fact that there's now just a handful of us only accentuates the void. I have so much spare time that I spend whole afternoons roaming the forest in the company of the dogs. Today we got as far as the electric fences, where the property runs up against a pair of enormous greenhouses. They're elegant box-shaped structures, rectangular skins of translucent plastic stretched over frames of metal and wood. The savanna is full of constructions like these; you can see them from the window of any approaching plane. My fondness for greenhouses is something I inherited from my father, who cultivated flowers and liked showing me where he'd made his fortune. Maybe a greenhouse was where I had my first impression of beauty: the uniformed women, masked and gloved, manipulating orchids first into cellophane packs and then wooden crates. Come to think of it, I can't recall seeing the face of a single one of those workers. I only remember naked eyes above masks. The gloved hands, the scissors, the movements synchronized as if in some kind of ritual. Nothing could be further from the idea of industriousness my father so fiercely defended, apart from the sweat on the worker's brow. If I could, I would cross the electric fence now, I would go inside the greenhouse. Through the translucent plastic I intuit the movements of bodies.

3

The directors come to see me at the lab to tell me how well the drug is selling. One of them scribbles something on a Post-it before sticking it on my forehead. I reach for it, but the other stops me, clicking his tongue and wagging one finger. Easy does it, he says, enjoy the suspense. I slowly peel off the Post-it, feel the adhesive dirtying my forehead: naturally, it's a very large number. The twins' doubled smile hangs in the warm office air. Best of all, our predictions were correct, says one mouth. The drug is a hit with all target groups. It's the only product stocked evenly across every point of sale.

4

Jumping around in the discoteca with number 4 and my wife. Jumping over and over beneath the strobe light. What if this is it? Could anything surpass this state of beatitude and prosperity? I live with two beautiful women who lavish me with everything I need; I slack off as much as I want to on the job and invent new products at my leisure, new and unprecedented drugs for all the world: cheap drugs, smart drugs, increasingly potent drugs that yield endless variations on human experience. And if it's true that my latest drug knows no class distinctions, that it works regardless of economic or educative rank, that means a certain kind of democracy is attainable via consumption. That's what my new feminist, egalitarian work seems to prove. Because my art, unlike my wife's, doesn't just unite the intellectual elite. My art is for everyone, for anyone, no previous study required, nor gifted interpreters of some hermetic language, no liturgy. The only field of legitimization is the market. Or, to be precise, the body and the market.

5

Are you happy? my wife asks. Yes, number 4 responds, I really like being here with you. The only thing I'm worried about is my daughter, she's at my mom's place, and I don't like leaving her there. My wife and I exchange a glance. This subject is off-limits for us. Any mention of children makes us intolerably uncomfortable. Number 4 must be testing us. Maybe she's hoping we'll give her the green light to bring the girl here but is incapable of asking directly, as if deep down she knows something like that would destroy everything, would be the end. In a few days I'll have to go get her and take her back home, she says, lowering her head. I can't tell if her anguish is genuine. For the rest of the afternoon, the women seem somewhat suspicious of each other. I have to resort to the drug to alleviate tensions. When the substance takes effect, we go to bed, problem solved.

6

We're on a walk in the countryside with one of my wife's colleagues, who breathlessly flatters number 4 in the same obsequious tone the aesthetes use to describe whatever thing, whether they like it or not. What an enchanting young woman, he says, attractive, intelligent, you couldn't ask for more. My wife senses my irritation and tries to redirect the conversation to the scenery; she talks about the purity of the streams in the high mountains, the precision with which all life is organized. She parrots her own mystic clichés—landscape, fire, solitude. My wife's colleague says some of his friends have gone to live in a mountain house with no electricity or running water. They grow their own food, they're completely self-sufficient, he says, independent, they don't need anything from anyone. They even make their own soap with recycled oil and animal fat. Number 4 looks around with cold interest. I don't think she ever learned to take pleasure in nature. And yet, her way of looking, the economy of her gestures, captivates me again, like in those early days at the lab, long before my wife decided we'd be a triangle, when number 4 was mine alone and I methodically transcribed her hallucinations. It's as if years have passed when it's only been weeks. The change is that drastic. Our exclusion from the talk of the pleasures of country life grants us a moment together again. I go to her and take her arm, as I did on those nights when we walked in the garden. She recognizes the touch, smiles, places her palm on my cheek. I kiss her softly on the mouth. My wife pretends not to notice, but even so she can't finish her sentence, becomes flustered, frowns. Stunned, her colleague begins to chatter on about some indigenous petroglyphs nearby, promising next time he'll take us to see them.

A few hours after the walk, we return to the country house for lunch. We eat carne asada and papas criollas, freshly baked country bread, queso paipa, and candied figs with dulce de leche. Over dessert, my wife and number 4 recover the thread of their complicity, and I am again alone. Outside one of those vaporous rains begins to fall, the kind you only see in the high plains. The green foliage gives off a shine that revives us, and cool gusts of living things come into the house to mingle with the scent of burning wood.

7

My wife has been reading a review of her show for some time. She reads it and, incredulous, reads it again. Now she's asked number 4 and me to listen to a few lines: "She manages something simply di*vine*: the reduction of any trace of radical gesture to a mere exercise in interior design. This woman believes she can create an artistic masterwork simply by taking refuge within her refined (read rarefied) taste, but in the end, comme ci, comme ça. Indeed, the staggering conceptual framework surprised me for its complete lack of congruency with the poverty of the visual language." Don't let it get to you, I say, all the other reviews have been positive, the ones that matter say the show was of the highest order. The ones that matter were written by my friends, she says, but the person who wrote this was being frank. They have nothing to lose. The person who wrote that is jealous of you, I say, it's obvious how resentful they are. My wife is upset. You just don't get it, do you, she says, you never get it. I could strike her for what she's just hurled at me; I look at her, enraged. But there's more. And she reads it aloud: "Sometimes brilliance like this astounds only for its stubborn uselessness." And again: "Sometimes brilliance like this astounds only for its stubborn uselessness." Who could have written that, she says, it's signed with a pseudonym. Number 4, who has withheld her opinion so far, intervenes to tell my wife that the critic makes a good point. Otherwise, number 4 says, you wouldn't be thinking about it so much. Maybe it's time for a change.

8

My wife continues to torment herself over the review. She doesn't want to go out; she spends all day in pajamas. The only things that improve her mood are the drug and, to a lesser degree, conversations with her new friend, who critiques her work without mercy. Number 4 offers advice even I wouldn't dare provide. My wife swings between excitement at the prospect of overhauling her process and anxiety at not knowing where to begin. Until yesterday I tried to insist on the fact that all the reviews, save for that one, had been positive. But my wife is obsessed with the idea of progress, and I fear she's in the wrong. In part because there's one thing the critic is right about, bad blood aside: my wife is incapable of abandoning the circle of comfort her good taste affords her. That fortress has been years in the making, stone by stone. It's her proudest accomplishment, the sensitive nucleus of her entire oeuvre.

9

Number 4 and I go to the grocery store. We try not to stray from the list my wife has provided and stroll along tossing items into the cart. What if the two of us lived alone, somewhere far away from my wife? The problem is, that plan would involve the child, too, and I'm not sure I'm ready for that. This was all supposed to be mere diversion, an accessory amusement, like taking a rare drug or discovering a new restaurant. Now I'm considering leaving my wife to run off with this stranger. What the hell is happening to me? In the dairy aisle, I attempt an inevitably clumsy declaration of love, during which number 4 tries to keep a straight face. Let's get out of here together, I say, us and the little girl. Her expression is inscrutable. Or maybe she herself doesn't know what to feel, and her face reflects a confusion that, in the end, resolves into cynicism. You don't know me, Doctor, she says. After that I insist, I implore, I don't know what stance to take, and all at once my words take on the entire spectrum of possible tones, a mixture that disgusts even me: arrogant, submissive, supplicating, authoritarian, clinical. Number 4 repeats: You don't know me, Doctor. And goes back to pushing the cart.

10

The directors came back to the lab today. What made this visit unusual was the pair of spider monkeys they brought into my office. For a moment I felt panicked, then I was amused. Allow me to introduce the new security team, the intellectual said. I thought they were joking and let out a loud laugh. The directors stared back at me very seriously. The scene was like something out of a nightmare: each twin in an impeccable suit, each arrogant face repeated with minimal variations, and in each pair of arms, a black monkey with sorrowful, aqueous eyes. The dogs and the system aren't enough, the intellectual went on. I made a final attempt to unmask the comedians, but there was no chance: they were serious. The dog people work with spider monkeys now, said the other, who usually does all the talking. Monkeys are much more versatile, they're silent, lethal, they might as well be little ninjas. And although by then I knew they weren't joking, I could only double over with laughter, which seemed to disturb the monkeys. Cool it, the intellectual ordered, that laugh is no good, it's making them nervous. Relax and give them your hand, make a good first impression or they might mistake you for the enemy. God forbid! I shouted, and burst into laughter again. The monkeys started howling as the directors tried to apply the calming techniques they'd learned from the trainers. They squeezed their necks gently and whispered *shhhh, shhhh.*

After lunch I went out for a walk in the forest, but heavy rain forced me back in after just fifteen minutes. I did nothing but stare out the window the rest of the day.

11

How could you have brought her to the opening, my wife, who is still wrapped up in the bedsheets, says through clenched teeth. She talks as if number 4 weren't listening from the other room. Where'd you get a twisted idea like that, tell me, where, to set that thing loose, let her prance around next to *my* pieces, wearing *my* dress. You're sick, you're *really* sick, you knew what that would do to me, you knew it would destroy me, you had it all worked out. The shouting rings out across the entire apartment. It makes no difference to me if my wife is upset, it'll pass, I'm sure. What does bother me is the fact that, after this little scene, number 4 will have to go. Calm down, I say just to say something, knowing my casual tone will only provoke her. And indeed, the demon is unleashed: You're jealous, she says, you're a toxic slug with no talent of your own, and that's why you're only happy watching the light in other people go out. You make me sick. You make me sick. . . . Suddenly I'm on the set of a telenovela, the substance of reality itself corroded by the absurd, the performance fractured from the very core of dramatic action. But that's life, I think, that breakdown's no error; it's encoded in the structure itself—of a catastrophic economy. I let her go on for a while, and when she's tired herself out, I suggest she take a dose. Now she's buried her head in a pillow, wailing like a spoiled brat. I don't want it, I hear her say, her voice a whisper muffled by down. I don't want your shit, I want nothing to do with it. And she goes on howling. But it will pass, that much I know. In a minute or two she'll resurface, strands of hair stuck in her mouth, makeup running from her eyes, and, face still contorted from sobbing, she'll ask for a pill.

12

When my wife falls asleep, I go out to the living room and number 4 looks at me, terrified. I never meant to cause you any trouble, she says, I'm so sorry, and she grabs the phone to call a taxi. I ask if she wouldn't rather I give her a ride. Number 4 presses her lips together and shakes her head. She probably spent all afternoon arguing with my wife. That won't be necessary, she says, it's better this way, and we sit in silence, holding hands on the couch. Five minutes later, the doorman calls to let us know the taxi is here. Number 4 grabs the small backpack she brought to the lab a few weeks ago. She gives me a long kiss good-bye, we hug, I grab her tightly by the waist. I'm driven to insist: I don't want you to go, I say, and my offer still stands, we could live together, just the two of us, with the child, of course. Those words sour the moment. She concludes the embrace, turns around, and walks out the door after refusing to give me any means of contacting her, neither address nor phone number. Call me, I yell as I watch her go down the long hallway. Do you have enough pills? I ask. And as she disappears into the elevator, her only discernible gesture is a slight nod. Then the hallway's automatic lights go out, but I can't close the door. Instead, I stand for some time in the threshold, summoned by the darkness, which, along with the dizzying void of the architecture, seems to want to suck the life from my body.

13

Lacking obligations, I spend all week in the lab reviewing the four participants' files. I rewatch the videos taken while the women were on the drug. There's no audio, so I can only study number 4's gestures as she makes her pronouncements. Her path through the room describes a clockwise elliptical pattern, though she occasionally pauses to crouch and examine the floor as if leaning over a pond. I'm compelled to reread the transcriptions several times in a row and only stop when I realize obsessive rereading is a sign of frustration.

To clear my head, I go for a walk in the garden, trailed closely by the two monkeys. They move on all fours, steps synchronized, taking everything in with endearing expressions of permanent awe. You'd think they were rediscovering the world again and again. Their motions are so cadenced and graceful, everything in their body language seems so essential, that for a moment I'm tempted to believe there were no errors or adjustments in their evolutionary design. That walk transmits a strange sensation of perfection. It's true, they are little ninjas.

The dogs bark in the distance. I wonder how the dogs and the monkeys get along. Did the two idiots even consider that?

Once I've entered the pine forest, the monkeys scale the trees and survey the area for possible threats. They really are well trained. I sit down and recline against a tree trunk. The dogs are still barking, and I'd like to go see them, but I'm afraid an encounter between the four animals could end in catastrophe. I fantasize about walking the premises surrounded by dogs and monkeys. My father never let me have pets. He said they feminized the character. The closest I ever came to one was the anthill I staged in a glass case at my high school science fair, a prosperous microsociety that, in spite of its markedly militant and manufactural qualities, failed to win my father's approval. Don't be a pansy ass, get rid of it, he said when I still had the case in my room weeks after the fair had ended. Come to think of it, maybe my father was so opposed to the anthill because he intuited that inside, a splendid matriarchy was being established, under the rule of an idle queen whose sole enterprises were procreation and being fed by her creatures.

Suddenly the first drops of what's bound to be a great down-pour begin to fall, so I stand and return to the lab, where the transcriptions, the videos of number 4 to be watched in slow motion for the nth time, the minuscule details of that kabuki of mute gestures all await. Later, when the walls of my office cast back the first flashes of lightning, I go to the window. Outside, the thick, leaden afternoon and, at the foot of the building, next to the fountain, the pair of monkeys, standing guard despite the downpour. It makes me a little sad to see them that way, soaking wet and motionless as gargoyles. The dogs bark and go on barking. Following an inexplicable impulse, I grab my umbrella and go out to the garden. The monkeys make as if to follow me, but I shout at them to stay where they are. Surprisingly, they obey and recover their pathetic immobility. I take the gravel path toward the front gate, afraid I'll be met with a nasty surprise, that the dogs will be sick or injured. I drag that bad premonition along, brooding beneath the umbrella, swerving to avoid puddles and patches of mud.

Seeing the animals safe and sound in their kennel fills me with puerile joy, but I don't think to be ashamed of it. I'm relieved to confirm that the dogs are unharmed, that their kennel has sheltered them from the storm, and I almost weep with joy when I kneel to pet them and they wag their tails.

14

This morning I called one of the directors to ask if there's a henchman available. I'll send one over now, he said. A few hours later, a guy who looks like a henchman walks into my office, a bad caricature with a pockmarked face, yellow-green eyes, and a military haircut. What can I do for you, Doctor? he says, and his voice, sweetly obedient, complicates his villainous appearance. I need to find out where someone lives. I give him photos and facts. The guy doesn't ask any questions; he's a professional, just like the monkeys. Now it's only a matter of time.

15

My wife still won't get out of bed. To make matters worse, she's cycling between my drug and lines of cocaine. Days pass as she watches TV in a trance. Sometimes she stands up, euphoric, grabs a notebook, starts to draw. Balls of crumpled paper accumulate near the bed, alongside some very remarkable drawings that look like electrical circuits or the skeletons of reticular machines. We don't exchange a word. I begin to feel sorry for her, to miss her cheerful disposition, her intelligence. Our old, spent love sends out flares in the distance: a shipwreck.

16

This morning the monkeys captured an owl I'd seen circling the forest for days. And they brought it to my office. An offering, I guess. Since the cleaning staff is scarce, I had to wait a long time for them to come and collect it. The image of the dying bird, still flapping around at the foot of my desk, the little monkeys skipping to and fro in celebration—in short, a chain of bad omens. I've always been a bit superstitious, but let's admit that lately, strange things have been happening, signs that hardly bode well. And then, just this afternoon, one of the directors calls, the more talkative one. He asks if everything's going O.K. here, if I've noticed anything out of the ordinary. I tell him about the owl. Nothing else? he says, so it's understood that the owl doesn't seem like much to him. Nothing else, I say, why do you ask? The director clears his throat uncomfortably. Nothing to worry about, but there's been a hell of a disturbance in one of the heavyweight slums down south. You know what those places are like, he says. But the truth is, I have no idea what those places are like. They say there are whole streets dedicated to the distribution of every imaginable vice, like a great market, that there are hundreds of small stalls built from scrap metal and plywood. I've seen some footage on TV.

The manager explains that a band of women addicted to the new drug organized a riot to sack the house of one of the suppliers. Apparently they stole around twelve hundred pills. The women broke into the guy's house armed with revolvers, knives, machetes. And yesterday, he says, our supplier took his boys out to comb the whole area, and, well, you can imagine what happened next. Those idiots got so carried away the police had to intervene. They told me around fourteen women are dead.

17

I had to leave the car at the mechanic, so I'll be taking a taxi around for the next few days, a completely different, and perhaps richer, experience than driving through the city alone. I don't know what our taxi drivers did to get such a bad name, they're no worse here than anywhere else. The poor things are stigmatized. The driver who takes me into the lab this morning is very funny, he gives a running commentary on the morning news. Suddenly they're talking about the slum, about the disturbances and the fourteen women killed. But the driver's good mood doesn't flag, even as they recount the brutalities. I listen closely, but they make no mention of the new drug, alluding instead to a settling of scores between two rival gangs. The driver, however, is fully informed. Sounds like the ladies are pretty worked up about some new pill, he says. It's a wicked one. Gets them all hot and bothered, haven't you heard? No, I say, then I ask him to tell me more, and he gives me the details: how they broke into the supplier's house to steal the pills, how they shamed him while his four bodyguards looked on. The fracas took them all by surprise, he says, nobody had time to turn around, they caught the poor kids with their pants down! The driver looks in the rearview mirror and goes on: And sir, you know how the women in this country get when they want something, just look at those lady guer-rillas, and the paratroopers too, they're the toughest in com-bat, I bet you had no idea. I'll tell you something: Colombian women are worse than any son of a bitch around. In this country, the old broads are the ones giving orders, they keep us boys under their thumbs, they can make us and break us. And now, with those pills, shit, I don't even want to imagine, all of them mad as hell. If it were up to me, I'd keep them on a short leash.

Business continues as usual at the lab. The only news is that the monkeys and the dogs are now getting along. I take an afternoon stroll through the forest with all four animals. Surrounded by beasts, I feel like a walking Saint Francis of Assisi prayer card. The henchman calls to tell me he hasn't managed to find anything out about number 4. It's like the earth has swallowed her whole, he says.

18

The driver who takes me back home that night is a serious, gaunt man who seems to prefer silence. He's the type that keeps the radio blaring and speeds down empty streets. I lean back against the seat and enjoy the velocity. The city comes through the window in a string of wet, wasted things, in sheaves of tepid light and broken symbols all along the cemetery wall, a kind of ideological border left out in the cold. My wife would be repulsed by how much graffiti there is around here. There's also a good view of the hills, implied as thicker shadows beyond the buildings in the old financial center, which are now no more than forsaken relics of late-fifties Creole functionalism. There's something sinister about those square masses, some of which appear empty, though they're surrounded by high-rises with colorful ads projected on their façades. Those are the lights you can see from the lab window, when the pollution and the clouds allow them through.

When we arrive, I see the doorman of my building note the taxi's plate number in a register, which I find strange. What's this all about? I ask. The doorman explains that it's a security measure, company orders. With taxi drivers, you never know, he says, it's better to be safe.

My wife is still in bed, reading with the TV on, but her mood has improved, and not without reason. Today, the bald architect bought the two most expensive pieces in the show.

I brush my teeth, put on my pajamas, and get in bed next to my wife, who's absorbed in her crime novel. Once in front of the TV, I'm unable to keep my eyes open. I'm exhausted, though on this tedious day, I've done nothing but squander my energy thinking about the moment when I'll next see number 4.

19

In the middle of the night, something very urgent wakes me up. Maybe I'm still asleep, maybe this is a dream, but even so, the idea that has taken me out of bed subdues me, drags me outside the apartment, and compels me to take the elevator down. In the lobby, I find the doorman dozing in a position that seems highly inconducive to rest. It's a mystery how he stays in his seat. The poor fellow wakes with a start and apologizes. Let me see the taxi register, I say. Then, almost without further effort, I locate the date, time, and plates.

20

I've spent the last few hours anxiously waiting at the lab, looking out the window every now and then. At some point mid-morning, the henchman arrives in the company of an older gentleman who says he owns the taxi. I ask if he remembers taking a woman somewhere a few days ago, show him several photos, recite my address. The gentleman perfectly recalls both number 4 and the place where he dropped her off.

The henchman offers to come along. I'd prefer to go alone, I say. He insists, assures me that the neighborhood we're headed to is very dangerous, but I check him with one look. Why don't you just let me know if you find out anything else, I say, modulating my hostile tone. The henchman shrugs and leaves.

21

An hour later, the taxi climbs a very steep hill toward one of those neighborhoods that hang off the side of the low eastern mountains, a single crush of old houses and ruins occupied by what my father called the guacherna and which I used to imagine as ghost or mythical creature. So many years later, the word *guacherna* has come to suggest no more than a shapeless ball of cultural debris. We stop before a metal gate painted green. I'll wait for you here, sir, the driver says. There are people streaming up and down the hill, child workers, women with crates full of vegetables, kids without prospects who, if they're lucky, will turn into thugs. I ring the bell two, three times, and nothing. The driver suggests I wait in the car, but just then I hear the bolts begin to slide back, the keys turning in the locks beyond. I'm so nervous my temples throb. The door opens, and I'm met with number 2's rococo mask. The surprise is mutual. Her sausage lips on my cheek do little to allay my disbelief.

22

The woman invites me in through a very long hallway, grabs my hand, and continually turns to smile at me, she saunters ostentatiously, smirks at the curious tenants who come out to get a look at the guest of the richest woman in the entire house, the entire neighborhood. We cross a patio filled with plants. Instead of pots, they've been planted in paint or fuel cans sawed in half. Next there's another long hallway, where the curious emerge in increasing numbers—children, old people, women, some of whom number 2 greets warmly, others she doesn't acknowledge, we turn right then left, we're going in circles, maybe in spirals, I'm lost, can't make sense of the shape of this house, another patio, another hallway, a bathroom, a wall lined with birdcages, someone is frying something, the odor of lard, a door opening to a windowless room, an enormous armoire and mirror, photos stuck to the walls and the ceiling, the bed unmade. Both of us know what's going to happen; it happens. She closes the door behind me, unzips my pants. I feel my eyes twitch as she sucks and sucks with all her impossible face, which expands and contracts, which seems to run then congeals again, because she looks at me as she does it, and I look back so she knows that, without even knowing it, I wanted this from the start, since the moment I saw that monstrosity of a face, which I collapse into, which isn't the threshold of any body since now there is only body or only head, there is no way in or out of any body, her breasts are two heads that can only look inward, above a navel that seems to be muttering something, then me, extension or adornment, just a graceless bit of gaud, a perplexed accessory emerged from the mouth of that vast and centerless face.

23

I don't have any, I say. Number 2 wants a dose. She's gone days without one because, according to her, the prices surged after the disturbance in the south. We're in bed staring up at the ceiling, plasterboard panels covered in clippings from magazines. What is all that? I ask, pointing. Number 2 says they're things she really likes: celebrities, body parts, a muscular leg, a slender arm, a delicate hand with perfect nails, a designer bag, a dress, a hat, a perfume. You really didn't bring me even one little pill? she asks. She gives me a sly look that, like everything else about her face, seems exaggerated. Just like you're not really here for me, are you? she says. I shake my head and ask what she knows about number 4. Not much, she says, she showed up here and asked if I had room for her. I couldn't have been her first choice, I mean, we don't really know each other. I gave the other girls my number and address just to be nice, mostly hoping they'd start coming to the salon. When she turned up, she said she needed a place for three nights. I said, No problem, honey, stay as long as you need, but the next day she left without saying bye, took off before I even got up for work. I ask if she left a note, an address, a phone number, anything. Number 2 gets out of bed and comes back with a bag containing a toothbrush, dirty underwear, and an unmarked newspaper. We sit in silence, and when she notices I've become limp handling the objects in the bag, number 2 climbs on top of me. How about another go? she says.

24

I wake up with no idea where I am, then, little by little, the hideous features surface: eyelids with fake lashes like barbed wire; enormous, introspective tits. The reprise was even better. I look at the old clock radio on the nightstand, six p.m. I get up very slowly, not wanting to wake her, and try to dress without making any noise, but she opens her eyes and smiles. Leaving already? she asks. Yes, I say, it's late. The woman gets up and puts on a shabby silk robe whose colors, at one point, were vibrant. I'll walk you to the door, she says, and we leave the room to retrace the entire spiraling labyrinth, which reveals new details in reverse: a wall decorated with pictures of saints; an empty henhouse, its floor smeared with feathers; a fish tank collecting dust beside the remains of several bicycles; a concrete tub where a woman scrubs her sheets. When we get to the front door, number 2 tells me to come back whenever I like, that I'm always welcome, but that next time I have to bring her some escargot. Escargot? I ask. Yeah, escargot, she repeats. That's what they're calling the pills, but I really have no idea why. They also call them biscuits, misties, scorchers, minnows, golden crisp, pocket triangles, snatches, flip-outs, poofs. . . . Wait here while I call you a taxi, she says.

25

From the office window, columns of smoke, so far off they appear minuscule, rise from the raided neighborhoods. There's a helicopter circling over the dry southeastern mountains, where the situation appears to be gravest. The directors say bands of women everywhere are organizing to raid any supplier they can find; a few groups have already managed to amass their own caches, which include a good amount of stolen merchandise and arms. The police and the suppliers' boys are trying keep the sales zones under control, but things are getting ugly. One director, the intellectual, suggests we take the pills off the market for a few weeks, just until the waters calm. The other doesn't want to be so drastic; he'd prefer to withdraw the product from the peripheral neighborhoods and hike up the price so only women with money can afford it. The intellectual tries to hide his irritation as he explains to his brother that if we were to do that, the gangs would waste no time in coming for the rich. And from there we'd be a step away from the whole enterprise going to shit, he says, and takes a sip of water while stroking one of the monkeys. They ask me what I think, if I have any ideas, but I'm distracted by what's happening outside the window: the garden is full of armed thugs, just like in the narco shows. Because when all's said and done, that's what we are: narcos, straight out of the movies. We're guacherna, every last one of us.

ECONOMY 2

What Number 4 Said When No One Was Listening

I arrive at the house, admire the house, a beautiful house that belonged to my father until my mother's husband took it over. My mother's husband was a front man for my father, was the one who showed up on most of my father's property deeds, though they did what they could to get rid of him, my father had a steady hand, but my father wasn't a butcher like the ones who came for him later, wasn't a butcher like me, who will do what I've done already and what now cannot be undone. Some things one does before doing them, I arrived at the house, I admired the house, the one that, of all the houses, my mother liked best, and with everything planned, everything measured, today is the day, I'll do it, I already have. Some things are already done, works of art aren't produced but fulfilled, like a prophecy, the effects unknown at the outset, they're actions in the purest sense, no end but the action itself, and when the work is complete, the action complete, the thing's time has come. The thing is what dies, the thing is what's spent, what erodes, and from there, the useless sensation of beauty, the ornamental effect, what lasts, the living fossil of action. Because there's no thing without action. The action, however, doesn't require the thing, the action can do without it. I arrived at the house, I admired the house, everything already done, the house a mere receptacle for the action: the house will be the thing, I said, the house the living fossil, the sleeping fossil of unflinching action. I came alone, where could the kid be, the kid isn't here, she's gone, I'm alone, don't have the money, either, today, won't be able to pay what I owe, the kid's hospital visit, an arm and a leg, the kid's treatment, an arm and a leg, still, I haven't shown up empty-handed, I've got the tool, the medium for the oeuvre, my action will be simple, elegant like a straight line, straight, and what's left will be an arm and a leg, a dormant source of forms amid chaos, an arm and a leg and an eye where, in the garden in ruins, nocturnal animals go to drink water, she likes to receive us this way so we can admire her, likes us to take in her beauty, which endures, which lasts and lasts like the living dead, she likes to be the thing in the house, the house in the thing: for a time, the houses were built in accordance with stylish prototypes, neoplasticism, functionalism, rhinoplasticism, rational tropicalism, my mother, tropical beauty, reaper of sighs, captain of spasms and strangleholds like a long, endless hallway, no windows or doors, and she must be as old as this house, both would be vintage beauties if not for the front man, who drove them to ornamental abuse, to gratuitous swapping of parts, antifunctional, dead reticulum fastened to cornice, ass, wall, or chest, the bombastic brow painted like trompe l'oeil, my mother naked on the floral quilt, My grandma is so pretty, said the kid, I hear her voice say My grandma is so pretty, like a doll, and it's true, my mother looks just like a doll, a flesh-and-blood doll fresh from the box, not a single spare fold of skin, a really good surgeon trims them all off, and she has no hair anywhere either, and her vulva, shaved smooth, is the absolute affirmation of ornament, the absolute negation of the house's architectural austerity, its design comprised entirely of smooth surfaces, straight lines, long ellipses interrupted by more straight lines, further obstructing the view of the infinite cavity, the crease, the thing negating the thing in eternal suggestion of something that never appears, until one arrives at the house, climbs the stairs, and sees Mom on the bed, naked on the floral quilt, the dynamism of her form at first suggests continuity with the architecture, but then her incredibly smooth vulva appears, perfectly hairless, monstrous in its infantile tidiness, so sinister in its resemblance to the kid's, there it is, like a shard of indigenous pottery, an unexpected arabesque that cancels every space in a thing that only admits the necessity of creating them all, all spaces unfold from the cunt, and so the house emerges from the depilated thing, the perennial grimace revealed, and the problem is, after so many surgeries, god knows why, she's developed a very rare skin allergy and twice a day has to be slathered with creams. Everything completes, even her words: Be good, now, honey, put a little cream on me. I smear my mother's body with creams. She closes her eyes, demands adoration, allegiance. My hand, tracing the body, under the watch of the grimace, which will soon take its place beside arm and leg and eye and house as another emblem, something recognizable in an unrecognizable mass. The face executes what will be its final movements, within seconds those very movements will be impossible, destroyed along with the rest of the mask. My mother and I are alone in the house, my first love, the front man with hair dyed red like a squirrel's, went out early, we're alone, alone for the first time in so long, the kid who joined and divided us gone, for a time the kid broke the perverse symmetry of the double, until there wasn't a kid anymore, thereby leaving my mother and me alone in the house, a pair of redundant objects reciprocally disavowing each other and flowering in that hatred, like two old political parties secretly sharing a bed in the ministerial sewers, my mother and I alone and soon to be one, rid of artificial separation. The thing completed, I incarnated her preterit beauty and even betray signs of future aging, like in a fairy tale, I'll be my mother in me, through me, she and I, no I left separate from her, I'll die wearing my mother's face, and therefore it's up to me to say who I was before I open the jar, now that my mother's eyes are closed in pleasure, open the jar of innocent liquid having smeared her with creams, who was I, another kid who couldn't sleep and walked the house at night, listening for sounds from other rooms, open the jar and scatter the innocent liquid over the face, erase a face, just like in a fairy tale, like in a telenovela, erase the witch's face, the wicked old woman's face, be sure to really burn just one eye, leave the other intact, the source of all forms, where the creatures go to drink water, the eye like a precious piece of black porcelain, now I, too, am naked, meanwhile, meanwhile, on the bed, the transformation occurs, I have to be naked to complete the transformation, my mother opens her mouth in a last attempt to hold on to her face as it dissipates amid screams no one hears, no one hears a thing, the house, the design of the house, its materials, the shapes of walls and ceilings extinguish the echo, isolate us acoustically from the outside world, my naked body dampens the screams, suppresses them as if it's all velvet, the noise enters my body and kills it, my body dies, my mother gets out of bed and runs to the door, but the door is locked, the key is in my hand, and her pain is my pain, she understands that my pain is hers, the pain is the key that can pass through our locks, the open mouth is a lock. I put on my mother's floral robe, now that my mother is on the floor, almost unmoving, resigned, no longer struggling,

I put the key in the lock and open the door, go down to the room below, where the cases are filled with figurines, down the stairs, one step, then another, another, It's over, I think, it's over, it's done, I touch my nose to make sure it's still there, Calm down, I say, it's mom's old nose, the nose you could touch as a little girl without worrying it would fall off and the skull underneath would show through, It's you, it's your nose now, take it away, the silk of the robe burns my cold skin. I was going downstairs when I saw the man of my dreams, the man who, back then, didn't dye his hair red like a squirrel's but slicked it with pomade instead, all the men who surrounded my father were ugly, unpleasant people, I was fourteen and everyone said that I was more beautiful than my mother, and my mother insisted I correct the minor defects, convinced me I needed adjustments, I was fourteen and I wanted to be more beautiful than my mother, and my mother pretended to mark the path to beauty when in fact her intention was to embody everything beautiful, the danger of life-long beauty, like the evil witch in a fairy tale, and she said: That doesn't go with this, how about a little lift here, why not have that bump filed down, fix your posture, your neck is too long, don't play that pretty face up too much or you'll just look like a giraffe, the giraffe was descending the stairs, measuring each step to avoid looking like a giraffe, to conceal the disproportion my mother continually pointed out, those spindly arms, that neck, all my father's men were ugly animals like me, faces like toads, like guinea pigs, faces like boars, we were very alike, they and I, we were disproportionate animals, they didn't dare touch me no matter how much they wanted to, and the man with the slicked-back hair stood out among them, the only one without animal features, a man straight out of a telenovela, beautiful. My mother was in favor of the match, told me I should prepare to become a real woman, she herself lied to my father so the slick-haired man could take me home with him. I loved the slick-haired man, the slick-haired man performed his task well, he was the front man, the actor from a telenovela, had no talents of his own but could fill in for anyone, was no one at whatever cost, devoted himself to the simulation of life, he was a coward, I was fourteen, and I liked that this much older man had noticed me, and my mother's complicity made the adventure more exciting, I went downstairs, saw him, and felt my stomach turn, writhe like a snake. That man was my lover, I had to remind myself on my way through the empty office at the back of the ground floor of the house, its walls covered with diplomas in accounting, statistics, and economics churned out by garage universities, a bookcase with books bound in dark-green leather, a photo of my mom in front of the Twin Towers, the office of the front man, who's now a nasty old geezer with hair like a squirrel, repulsed whenever he touches my mother, a disgusting, self-satisfied pervert who only goes to bed with little girls, and everyone knows, but my mother pretends that she doesn't after having done what she did to me. I don't know how long it's been since I was last at my mother's house, maybe months, I don't know, nor do I remember when the kid wasn't with me anymore, one day she was gone and my mother and I went back to being alone, like when I was fourteen and we shut ourselves up in my room and she asked me to tell her the details of my relationship with the front man and gave me advice on how to attend to him, what I should let myself do and how I should do it, and it didn't strike me as strange that she knew just what the front man liked, my mother knew these things, she was my beauty teacher, and she said again and again: You have to know how to make a place for yourself. And from that basic phrase hung all class of adornments: you have to know how to make a place for yourself, how to act, how to pose, how to laugh, when to cry, when to insist, when to beg, do it all at the opportune moment because a real woman is one who dominates feigning submission, submits feigning dominance, so the man never knows where to put himself, on top or on bottom, and you might be the one on your knees, but make sure he knows there are teeth in that mouth, that drives them all crazy, he'll be begging you for it, then you're in charge, you're the one who knows, that's what I learned from my mother, who always insisted I study a lot, insisted I get good grades. I don't want you to end up like me, she would say, I never had the chance to study, and look how I turned out. You have to study, get to the top of your class, go to college, get a degree, and then you'll be better than me, you'll be the prettiest girl *and* the cleverest, you'll know exactly how to handle men, how to beat them at their own game, the professional one, in offices, hallways, and conference rooms, men tremble in the face of a woman who knows, who thinks. My mother drilled studying into me. She read a lot, some of everything, without any hard rules, and she taught me to do the same from a very young age, Read, she would say, you have to read, don't go to bed today without reading, there are so many books in this house, you have so much to choose from, education comes first, you have to know how to make a place for yourself. And in part she mounted her little scenes to teach me things, once there was a group of characters with wigs and livery and embroidered dresses, tiny glass courtesan figurines. The characters formed a circle around a life-sized red crab. The scene was called Voltaire and his friends, my mom said. Who's Voltaire, I asked. And my mom explained that Voltaire was a

99

French philosopher, and then she explained who his friends were and what France meant, since I didn't know yet because I was still young and hadn't done any traveling, except to my father's properties in the countryside, or the coastal city where we vacationed once. You need to know more, said my mother, always arranging figurines in glass cases, always showing me things: This one here is Bolívar, she'd say, pointing to a little lead soldier, and this one is Manuela Sáenz, patriot, intellectual, and revolutionary. You have to be better than the men, the ones who show up in the books are all men, everyone knows who Bolívar is and thinks Manuelita was only his whore, they have no idea how much better she was than him, and that can't go on any longer. You have to study, better yourself, come out on top. There's no use for the uneducated woman anymore, stand out, get to know the enemy early, and that way they can't surprise you, because disillusionment is the heart of power, and at the heart of disillusionment is love, which is an impossible feeling, which never comes to anything. Be the first one to the heart of the heart of the heart and you'll understand the way this world works. Only the gullible fall in love, everything has its price, that's true, but there's always someone setting the prices, and that's the someone who's educated herself, education is the key, and don't you forget it. And I was a little girl, six years old, I stayed up late reading in bed and then went down to the glass cases to shine a flashlight on the figurines, to contemplate what my mother had said. A universal culture in glass cabinets. The world was mine. Thank you, Mommy, thank you for teaching me so much. I love you, Mom. You made me the woman I am. Now I have to go downstairs to complete the transformation. We're a unique and unnameable thing. You'll be the thing in the house, the remainder, and I'll leave the house and never come back. A long time ago I swore I'd never come back, but I came back. I still didn't know how to tell myself apart from you, which is why in the end I brought the kid with me, why after so many years spent drifting from one place to the next, the kid and I came back, and you were generous, you opened your home to me, lent me your money, rented a place for us so the kid and I could live well. I came back because I had no one to turn to, the kid was sick. I was afraid the kid would turn into your student too. That you would condition her at every opportunity then hand her over to the man with squirrel hair. The kid broke our symmetry, covered it up. When the kid was gone, I understood how we would separate, how we would stay together, more together than ever. And things began to take shape on their own, what started as almost an afterthought, an irresponsible spark of imagination slowly gaining form, the action negotiating to meet with its consummation, the action wanted to self-destruct at the moment of its completion, becoming a fixture in my life, giving meaning to time spent in preparation and the wait. I was methodical, scholarly, as I recalled the events that leveled a path for the action, I never got desperate, I went to the heart of the heart of the heart and found a loop of hatred, Mom, a hatred that wasn't yours or mine, but a hatred for the cosmic beginnings of femininity, a misogyny that exceeded the narrow confines of social psychology and acquired geological proportions, the world hates the feminine, I understood, convinced I'd struck a vein of precious meaning not meant to be exploited by anyone the way we women are. You screamed and those screams that couldn't escape the house somehow did escape the house, inside me, with me, you in me, Mom, together from now on, the two of us alone in me, your primal scream, telluric and surging from the thing, abandoning the house, in me, in you. I don't know when I left the house, don't know if the front man's boys are still searching for me. I've been hiding in plain sight, in one place or another, where it wouldn't occur to them to look. The front man can only simulate thought, he can't think for himself, my mother did all his thinking for him. Now there's only one refuge where no one will come looking for me, the eighth floor of a monumental old building, centrally located, right in plain view and passed over by everyone. Twice before I've hidden here. This is where they erected those massive cubes decades ago, to simulate a financial center for the modern city. There were offices in this building, and suites for whatever bankers, stockbrokers, profiteers, crooks passed through. But that was a long time ago, now the building's in disuse, though its owners must be raking in cash without lifting a finger, just letting it sit here and fall to pieces, now that the building is empty, I mean, now that no one is working or living here, because I'd be lying if I said it was empty, the building is full of things: in some offices there are filing cabinets crammed with documents, IOUs, policies, letters, reports, contracts, there are piled-up typewriters, poorly designed pieces of furniture, calendars from '74, '72, '65, letterhead for an insurance company, an investment group, a PR firm, prayer cards, photos of another era's politicians, old newspapers and newspapers and newspapers that seem to be written in another language. That keeps me busy. All of it needs to be sorted, objects arranged in each cubicle, office, and hallway. It's about mounting scenes with what's here, following a purely gratuitous pattern of shapes, sizes, no motivation but the carrying out of the action beyond its completion, a coda. Another woman gave me the idea, a very intelligent woman, admirable in many ways but nevertheless a prisoner of her upbringing. To say nothing of her husband, poor bastard, a monster, yes, but still, a poor bastard who sees the world from behind the bars of his upbringing. The hardest thing is to free yourself of an upbringing, I did all this to rid myself of it, and I'm still not sure I've succeeded, maybe this was part of my upbringing, maybe the sense of completion is in fact only the apex of my upbringing. In any case, I'm not finished yet, I have to draw the coda, the suspension points. The building an afterword made from existing materials: a desk, a chair, a broken windowpane, bullet casings (someone's been doing target practice), old publicity one-sheets for the banks and corporations. That's how I spend the day. Too much work for just one person. Too many floors, too many offices, too many objects to drag around on my own. I calculate that the work will be done in a few weeks. I still have money, they paid me well as a guinea pig. And I have pills enough to last me several days. Very rarely, I go to the grocery store for food, for jugs of water. Sometimes I go out just for a walk, I start walking wherever the most people are, comfortable in the chaos, less alone among others like me, wandering around as if we're not all just excess, as if we're all mysteriously vital, abandoned, vacant, crumbling faces. People move along uttering numbers, ciphers, the streets have no names, and therefore, the fate of the streets matters to no one, they only have numbers, and numbers say little or nothing. A city can't be talked about without names, it's impossible, it's all been worked out so the story stays neatly inside the mute numbers, and in the cabalistic intersections every corner generates, an arm comes out from underneath the shadows, just an arm asking for some spare change for the love of god, I let myself be swept along by the numbers, which seem emancipated from any arithmetic, abandoned numbers, just like us, I let myself be carried, and alien bodies go passing me by, the aromas, the clothing of secretaries and white-collar workers seeming to walk on its own, a parade of failed elegance, impossible elegance, unattainable and, anyway, out-shone by the authentic grace of people like me, who outfit themselves in everyone else's debris, I let myself be carried and see it take shape, the allure of some other glass case, the alter-native crevices offered up by the city, begging, insanity, vice, prostitution, like so many other consumer choices, things that are, in essence, inseparable from the lives of the rich, with their own rich-person things in their own glass cases, the ugly things around here being only imitations, doubles, and, at the same time, one with the rich-person things, like my mother and me, now that we'll never part. Then I remember my work isn't done, I'm missing the coda, the furniture and objects in the building must miss me, now that they're being looked after, it's best to keep close to the building, not stay outside for too long, I can't let them catch me before I'm done, the time will come when we decide what to do, Mother, don't worry, we'll do what's best for the two of us, but for now, we have to go back, retrace the path, unwalk it backward, review our aes-thetic choices, criteria ripened at last, mentally count up the money that's left, pass through the crowd, through the hole only you and I know, there, where no watchman will think to look, and although it's very late, it doesn't matter what time it is, doesn't matter that we're in complete darkness, we'll get to work, move things around, we'll stay busy doing our jobs.

CROOKED
SYMMETRY

1

The last few nights I've had a recurring nightmare in which I'm walking the grounds alone, a nightmare that varies minimally with each repetition, though the setting is always the same: the garden at the foot of the lab's colonial façade, the ghostly fountain, the perfectly linear trails leading to perfectly linear lawns with flower beds that, in the moonlight, reveal deeper colors, the benches where nobody sits, the trees dense with dark, shining leaves. Every leaf the shape and size of a mask, as if in answer to the row of four identically stoic owls gathered on the branches. The owls appear to whisper among themselves as they watch, watch over the promenade, like the owls in the old stories who warn or threaten or bear an ill-fated message. But on closer inspection, I realize the owls are simply devouring the fruit of the tree, a fruit that's brown on the outside and a shrill orange inside, fleshy like a mammee or a sapote. One of the half-eaten fruits falls at my feet. I pick it up to examine it and notice that there are fragments inside, bits of nails, hair, and teeth encrusted in orange flesh. I begin to pull them out with my fingers, and that's when I realize they're not external to the fruit but part of the fruit itself. Another day I dreamed that hunger drove me to devour the fruit, which tasted the way food gone bad in the refrigerator smells. Another, I dreamed the fruits fell to the ground and, once there, began to writhe like hairy rats, and then the owls feasted, falling upon their prey, which, when seized by the predators, let out piercing shrieks. The only thing that carries over from one version to the next is the end of the nightmare, the terrifying image that always ruptures the dream: number 4 emerges from behind a tree, fruit in hand, and walks toward me, smiling.

This time, I'm awoken by both the terror of the nightmare and another concern: What will become of the animals? I think, anxious over the fate of the dogs and the spider monkeys. It's too late to call the twins, but there must be someone monitoring the lab. I dial the main line and hear the voice of a man I don't know on the other end. I identify myself, ask him to patch me through to security. While the hold music plays, I try to reassemble a precise and dignified image of my circumstances: I'm lying next to my wife in a large wooden bed, in a country house her colleague has generously lent us, surrounded only by mountain sounds, far from the city, far from the lab. My wife, half-asleep, asks what I'm doing. I say nothing and hold up one hand. She turns over, drifting back off. The music stops. Hello, Doctor, good evening. It's the head of security. Anything new over there? I ask. Nothing at all, sir, everything's in order, we're still on watch. And the animals? Are they all right? Yes, they're fine, he responds automatically. Both dogs and both monkeys? I insist. Yes, of course, Doctor, they're very well trained, they never make a false move. There's no need to worry, sir, we'll die before they do, nothing will happen to them. I hang up.

I don't know why, but it terrifies me to think that something could happen to the animals, especially the dogs. I get up and go to the bathroom then drink two glasses of water in quick succession. My throat is dry; I must have been snoring all night. Through the house's large windows I can make out the dark countryside, the trees rocked by the wind. I get closer to the glass; something catches my attention. Far off, in a meadow, a very faint, diaphanous light seems to emanate from the ground. It's not the first time I've witnessed this phenomenon. When I was a child, my parents would take me to a country house in the heart of some towering mountains. It was cold, so it wasn't unusual for everything to remain half-covered in fog for the better part of the day, which means that, in my memory, I'm unable to reconstruct the shape of the house. In any case, it was big. The clouds would come down and cover almost half of it, devouring part of the roof. There was also a pool fed by a natural hot spring that filtered from a nearby volcano. We kids would swim in it and get out stinking of rotten eggs because of the sulfur and minerals. At night that same brightness would surface. We'd sit in the doorway and watch the light's vaporous dance with a deep sense of fear and respect. Once I heard the steward of the house say those lights meant there was a huaca down below, an old tomb surely replete with gold and little clay pots. He said the guaqueros who raided them knew how to read the lights, that just as some signaled gold, others signaled nothing. An unskilled guaquero would dig and dig and find only cow bones. Because sometimes it's the bones that shine, I remember him saying. And that's something I never forgot, that bones can glow in the dark. Several years later, leafing through an encyclopedia, I read about the luminous phenomena associated with ionization in a highly charged electric field, what the ancients knew as Saint Elmo's fire. Saint Elmo was the patron saint of mariners, who appealed to him when their ships' masts or lightning rods ionized during a storm and began to emit the notorious fire in the form of a bluish stream. That's how I knew it wasn't a lie: the bones ionize just like the masts, and they, too, can give off that strange light. Some animals' antlers do the same thing on nights like tonight, when there's high atmospheric electricity. After several days of sun and wind, the air signals the approach of a storm that is slow to arrive. I can sense it in the atmosphere and in my increasingly heavy sleep the last few nights. I've also noticed that the ionization affects my wife's body differently than it affects mine. During the day she's energized, powerful, and at night she sleeps like a log. I, on the other hand, can feel my hair standing on end at all times. But not from nerves, exactly, nor anxiety. It's something more profound. And maybe more literal, too, in the way the electrons at play in the atmosphere interact with my elemental particles. One day we'll discover how that phenomenon acts upon our bodies, what exactly it triggers, how it alters our behavior. But for now we can only speculate, still bound to superstition, observing the spectrum of brightness in the blue mist as it rises up from the meadow. Bones. My aching bones. Since we arrived over a week ago, we've spent most of our time walking increasing distances. The first day, on the suggestion of my wife's colleague, who owns the house, we hiked to a very steep cliff. The rocks were covered almost entirely in the petroglyphs of some vanished culture about which nothing is known, or so my wife's colleague said, very simple animal shapes and nested lines that form some kind of great labyrinth. I'm amazed by the intensity of the red, preserved across thousands of years. There's also, of course, the joker come to spray-paint his name on the rocks in blue, declare his love in pink, pay respects to his team in green. Guacherna, the damn guacherna.

Another day we got as far as an enormous reservoir, where we rented a little skiff. We sailed until lunchtime then ate trout at a grill on the shore. Lately we don't talk much, my wife and I. We're just together, without saying anything of significance, letting the time around us unfold. We've also visited several villages near the reservoir, all very small, each with its own church, tree-lined plaza, and police station.

Another day we crossed to the opposite end of the reservoir and walked to a different cliff, but this time, the petroglyphs were partially covered by paintings depicting religious scenes, various versions of the Marian apparition, kneeling parishioners. The destruction of the petroglyphs and the characteristics of the cliff face have made the place a sanctuary for climbers and extreme-sport enthusiasts: the rugged wall was stippled with carabiners, pickax scars, and ropes. My wife took an interest in the erasure of the petroglyphs. We asked around and eventually came to the tourism office, where we picked up some pamphlets explaining that a priest in the region, troubled by the proliferation of pagan cults around the petroglyphs, had ordered them covered by sacred images. The pamphlet absolved the priest of any guilt on the basis that times were different then, since all of this had taken place at the height of the Violence, when the struggle between liberals and conservatives obliged the latter to take desperate measures to thwart the spread of idolatry, communism, and freemasonry. Tear down the idols and raise the icons, my wife said after reading the pamphlet. We both laughed. We were sitting in the middle of a plaza in one of the pueblos. It was the only allusion to number 4 we allowed ourselves. We don't have the strength to discuss the matter, much less now that we know what she did. And it's not just a lack of emotional resources but also of intellectual ones: the thought of her makes us feel something akin to the glut of language. Today, as we crossed some already flowering potato fields on our way back from the reservoir, my wife said that what the priest did with the petroglyphs was a monstrosity, that there's no name for something like that. I shrugged, not caring to linger on the subject. An iconoclast, I said, like Moses. She gave me a very serious look, then confessed that she didn't remember Moses's iconoclastic episode and asked if I could please tell her how it went. I scoffed because my wife went to Catholic school. Tell me, she insisted. So I relayed the story as I remembered it. I talked about the debauchery of the people of Israel when Moses wouldn't come down from the mountain, which he'd climbed to receive the Ten Commandments. Moses had cleared them all out of Egypt, and without a leader to follow, they felt abandoned. Then Aaron ordered the people to collect all the women's gold earrings. With that gold and a burin, Aaron produced a gold calf, an idol the town worshipped with revelry and holocausts. God blew the whistle on Moses: The town has become corrupt, he said, they've abandoned the path I laid out for them, now I must unleash my wrath upon this unworthy people. And here comes the most incredible part of the story: Moses dares to criticize God's lack of consistency. He basically calls God an imbecile. Hey, cut it out, God, he says, I mean, you kicked these poor people out of Egypt, made me guide them across the desert, and now, just because of this minor detail, you're going to bump them all off? And Moses convinced God not to kill his people, and then he came down from the mountain and found everyone painting the town, all the people of Israel boozing it up around the gold statue. Moses went ballistic, and here comes another surprise: the guy is so mad he hurls the Ten Commandments to the ground and breaks them to pieces, the commandments written in God's very hand. Unwilling to stop at just crashing the Israelites' party, he grabs the golden calf and thrusts it into the flames, he stomps on it till it turns to dust, dust he scatters in water, water he makes all the Israelites drink. Do you believe it? He made them drink the water with gold dust from the calf made of women's earrings. By then, my wife was laughing hysterically at my version of the story. We went on that way for a while, laughing like idiots, laughter as release, laughter so we could forget about everything that's been happening to us. From time to time we stopped to admire the landscape and its details: a potato flower, a slug on a rotten trunk, a purple fungus. Later we started laughing again when my wife said that, compared to the twisted story of Moses and the calf, what happened with the priest and the petroglyphs almost seemed innocent, pastoral.

Bones. My aching bones. The long walk today tired me out. I need sleep. Now the bluish mist has been extinguished completely, there's no trace of it left in the air, everything's been restored to utter darkness. The discreet Saint Elmo's fire that shone in the field just a few minutes ago suddenly seems an impossibility; night recovers its vulgarity. Through the window I can make out the shapes of trees, a fence. My throat still hurts. I drink a third glass of water and lie back down beside my wife, who sleeps like a mummy.

2

The following day breaks with rain. The storm comes at last, thunder rolls. As we eat breakfast, already bored at the prospect of being trapped inside all day, I get a call from one of the twins, the more talkative one. He wants to know when I'm coming back to the lab. We've got everything under control here, he says, I mean, more or less, we're still on alert, but the worst of it's over, and we've got a hell of a lot of work to do on the generics. We needed you here yesterday, he says. I ask him how the animals are. Fine, fine, he says, I think they miss you, we all do, come quick, sweetheart, come quick. And give your wife a kiss for me, tell her my brother wants to come by the gallery to pick up a few little things for our mom. I hang up.

We finish breakfast in silence. And with nothing else to do, we lie back down to read, the mood thrown into confusion by the late night and gray weather.

Around noon it stops raining, the sun comes out, the sky clears. It looks like the weather will hold for the rest of the day. We eat some sandwiches and go out for our walk, but this time, instead of heading toward the reservoir, we take one of the paths that lead up into the mountains.

The humidity and the altitude make for a tiring ascent. We're obliged to stop and rest from time to time. I can hardly breathe, I've got a little tachycardia. But at least from here there's a very pleasing view of the whole valley: the reservoir and the little towns, the sheer cliffs on either side, the slivers of forest.

When we reach the summit, the terrain flattens into thick woodland. The walk becomes pleasant again, even leisurely, there's nothing strenuous about it. We're guided by the sound of a stream that hasn't yet appeared. We both decide it would be fitting to drink the fresh mountain water. My wife pauses occasionally to examine the orchids that grow among the mossy branches and stubble lichen.

After a while we come to the stream and drink until we're satisfied. We fill plastic bottles for what remains of the walk.

As we follow along the watercourse, a growing roar becomes audible. It's not long before we discover that the stream plunges over a wall of rock. From above we observe the cascade's trajectory, discern the laughter of women and music from a radio. Down below, in the well the water forms upon falling, there's a group of washerwomen in full furor. Some might call the spectacle repulsive: the women's bodies, robust from country labor, dancing cumbia and lathering one another up or obsessively wringing out sheets, but my wife and I know what that soap is capable of, to what lengths a woman might go under the influence of that soap. And besides, what we see down below doesn't seem grotesque to us, at least not in a pejorative sense. There's grace in what the women do with their bodies; in the dance, languid then frenetic; the constant improvisation, as if they're unable to separate work from play; in the laughter that flickers against the roar of the waterfall, transmitting joy. We shouldn't be spying on them, my wife says, let's go.

We take a different trail back down the mountain. We cross some pastures still wet from the morning's downpour.

My wife then asks why the twin called this morning. He wants me to go back to the lab right away, I say. She says nothing, but it's clear that the thought of being forced to return to the city irritates her. If she had her way, we'd settle here permanently, we'd take up gardening or oil painting landscapes and ecstatic country nymphs, like those early twentieth-century Austrian painters who, last I checked, we hated. Maybe I was wrong when I said my wife is incapable of renouncing her good taste.

3

That night I dream the same dream of the garden and owls. Fruits tumbling over the fallen leaves like rats. Tooth-encrusted flesh. I'm afraid of the end of the dream, I can see it coming now, I manage to stay narrowly ahead. And there she is: the woman in the green dress comes out from behind the tree with one of the fruits in her hand. She comes closer, smiling. The owls descend upon the rats. I master my fear, but I'm overwhelmed by the presence of the woman, who now plants herself before me, whose hair I can now smell, whose scent hurts. I'm going to laugh now, she says. And the sound of the words takes me by surprise. I wasn't expecting that, wasn't ready to hear her voice. The woman steps toward me, she opens her mouth, and I'm paralyzed. Her laughter enters the dream with such violence that it immediately shatters. I wake up and understand that it's my wife who is laughing, asleep with her back to me. In the darkness, I can only make out her long hair, a bulk that trembles lightly from the laughter. I can't tell if she's asleep. I place my hand on her head, but her head is no longer her head, nor her hair her hair, nor my hand my hand.

TRANSLATOR'S NOTE

The city has no name. It could be here, or anywhere. Its location in time isn't specified either. There's a faintly futuristic overlay, but the narrator's diction swings between antiquated formality and present-day slang, and, among other anachronistic details, there are both spider monkeys and henchmen on the security team. Characters, too, are referenced only by generic designation. "My wife," "the directors," "the taxi driver," "the architect." Even descriptive nouns of that kind are withheld from the study participants. They're granted only numbers.

The choice to leave these coordinates unfixed suggests universality, as if this same story might have played out (might be playing out) in any number of labs, in any number of cities. But it also enacts the social and political repression of a certain kind of anonymity. "A city can't be talked about without names, it's impossible," number 4 says. "It's all been worked out so the story stays neatly inside the mute numbers." How, *Ornamental* asks, do the nameless—disembodied voices, unattributed speech, figures "emancipated from any arithmetic"—participate in meaningful discourse, find a place among others, work toward common interest, tell their stories? And when do we encounter those stories, as readers who live in named cities and bear names ourselves?

Once, Juan pointed out that architecture can function as "a sculptural representation of failed futures." In this city scarred by absurdities, crises, injustices, our surroundings offer clues, to where we've been, to where we're going. There are "forsaken relics of late-fifties Creole functionalism" in the old financial center. The exploitative hacienda has been repurposed as an equally exploitative pharmaceutical lab. The "prodigious, lost-era" skyscrapers were abandoned "on the brink of rationalism." Buildings—their designs and locations, the condition they're in, what they replace and what they conceal—record histories and gesture toward one-time paths forward. Even the most "gleaming and beautiful" ones, the ones once symbolic of "prosperity" and "progress," recede into the unchanging chaos of the landscape, just as "yesterday's political discourses [become] today's collective unconscious." *Ornamental* can be read as a building can be read: as an object that records, with its highly stylized language and form, an interplay between ideologies. Its material details (language, texture, composition) tell us as much if not more than what would traditionally constitute plot.

A doctor's self-consciously formal discourse is interrupted at intervals by number 4's elaborate poetic outpourings. It's interrupted, but never wholly consumed. The doctor's wife, an artist whose works are overpriced "ornaments," is moved by number 4 to interrogate her practice, but only before fleeing back to the comfortable "fortress" of her taste. The excess, ephemerality, and exuberance of number 4's monologues are set alongside a sanitized and selective reality. They're the glints of the baroque against Loos's white walls. On the level of plot, the conflict is won by those walls—by rational, ordered discourse, smooth and functional surfaces, the conditions called for, in this case, by those who hold power. The novel ends not with any comforting resolution but with a return to the vortex of late capitalism. The scales tip back in the direction of privilege, or they never tip away. Evil can be observed but not upended; our irredeemable characters can't right a world gone wrong.

But that's not to say there's no relief. Because on the level of the sentence, there's still some room for astonishment: in the reactions sparked off when two lexicons are pushed up against each other, in the interplay of linguistic subtleties. There, the winner of this conflict doesn't seem to be determined from the outset. Because if education and upbringing are a prison, as *Ornamental* suggests, then so is language, which turns moments of rupture or linguistic difference into alternate paths of significance. When the study participants speak for themselves, contrasting styles puncture the doctor's grandiose and often classist rhetoric. Their survey responses are discrete poems that show what shape expression can take outside of narrow conventions. They're open to interpretation, vivid beyond the homogenizing constraints of grammar, unselfconscious and instantaneous. In these brief moments of potential, language that doesn't conform to certain imposed expectations proves as powerful and expressive as language that does. Both the doctor and his wife return to their lives of ease after number 4's departure. Both reassume the narratives they've carefully crafted for themselves. If number 4 has any visible or lasting effect on their lives, it may be only in the way the collar of the doctor's prose loosens, the naturalness and idiomatic expression it occasionally admits.

With whom do we empathize in such a book—a book described as an exploration of art's potential "for the examination of evil"? For our characters, there is no redemption, no lesson learned, no call to action. Each one is, as we are, "prisoner of [an] upbringing." And their world, like ours, is deeply flawed, deeply violent, deeply unjust. But with them, we see things we might not otherwise see, go places we might not otherwise go, witness our own circumstances drawn out to their logical conclusions. How do we look and listen from now on? Do the stories remain "neatly inside the mute numbers"? Perhaps, as readers, that's for us to say.

Lizzie Davis
NOVEMBER 2019

Coffee House Press began as a small letterpress operation in 1972 and has grown into an internationally renowned non-profit publisher of literary fiction, essay, poetry, and other work that doesn't fit neatly into genre categories.

Coffee House is both a publisher and an arts organization. Through our *Books in Action* program and publications, we've become interdisciplinary collaborators and incubators for new work and audience experiences. Our vision for the future is one where a publisher is a catalyst and connector.

Funder Acknowledgments

Coffee House Press is an internationally renowned independent book publisher and arts nonprofit based in Minneapolis, MN; through its literary publications and *Books in Action* program, Coffee House acts as a catalyst and connector—between authors and readers, ideas and resources, creativity and community, inspiration and action.

Coffee House Press books are made possible through the generous support of grants and donations from corporations, state and federal grant programs, family foundations, and the many individuals who believe in the transformational power of literature. This activity is made possible by the voters of Minnesota through a Minnesota State Arts Board Operating Support grant, thanks to the legislative appropriation from the Arts and Cultural Heritage Fund. Coffee House also receives major operating support from the Amazon Literary Partnership, Jerome Foundation, McKnight Foundation, Target Foundation, and the National Endowment for the Arts (NEA). To find out more about how NEA grants impact individuals and communities, visit www.arts.gov.

Coffee House Press receives additional support from the Elmer L. & Eleanor J. Andersen Foundation; the David & Mary Anderson Family Foundation; Bookmobile; Dorsey & Whitney LLP; Foundation Technologies; Fredrikson & Byron, P.A.; the Fringe Foundation; Kenneth Koch Literary Estate; the Matching Grant Program Fund of the Minneapolis Foundation; Mr. Pancks' Fund in memory of Graham Kimpton; the Schwab Charitable Fund; Schwegman, Lundberg & Woessner, P.A.; the Silicon Valley Community Foundation; and the U.S. Bank Foundation.

The Publisher's Circle of Coffee House Press

Publisher's Circle members make significant contributions to Coffee House Press's annual giving campaign. Understanding that a strong financial base is necessary for the press to meet the challenges and opportunities that arise each year, this group plays a crucial part in the success of Coffee House's mission.

Recent Publisher's Circle members include many anonymous donors, Patricia A. Beithon, the E. Thomas Binger & Rebecca Rand Fund of the Minneapolis Foundation, Andrew Brantingham, Dave & Kelli Cloutier, Louise Copeland, Jane Dalrymple-Hollo & Stephen Parlato, Mary Ebert & Paul Stembler, Kaywin Feldman & Jim Lutz, Chris Fischbach & Katie Dublinski, Sally French, Jocelyn Hale & Glenn Miller, the Rehael Fund-Roger Hale/Nor Hall of the Minneapolis Foundation, Randy Hartten & Ron Lotz, Dylan Hicks & Nina Hale, William Hardacker, Randall Heath, Jeffrey Hom, Carl & Heidi Horsch, the Amy L. Hubbard & Geoffrey J. Kehoe Fund, Kenneth & Susan Kahn, Stephen & Isabel Keating, Julia Klein, the Kenneth Koch Literary Estate, Cinda Kornblum, Jennifer Kwon Dobbs & Stefan Liess, the Lambert Family Foundation, the Lenfestey Family Foundation, Joy Linsday Crow, Sarah Lutman & Rob Rudolph, the Carol & Aaron Mack Charitable Fund of the Minneapolis Foundation, George & Olga Mack, Joshua Mack & Ron Warren, Gillian McCain, Malcolm S. McDermid & Katie Windle, Mary & Malcolm McDermid, Sjur Midness & Briar Andresen, Daniel N. Smith III & Maureen Millea Smith, Peter Nelson & Jennifer Swenson, Enrique & Jennifer Olivarez, Alan Polsky, Robin Preble, Alexis Scott, Ruth Stricker Dayton, Jeffrey Sugerman & Sarah Schultz, Nan G. Swid, Kenneth Thorp in memory of Allan Kornblum & Rochelle Ratner, Patricia Tilton, Stu Wilson & Melissa Barker, Warren D. Woessner & Iris C. Freeman, and Margaret Wurtele.

For more information about the Publisher's Circle and other ways to support Coffee House Press books, authors, and activities, please visit www.coffeehousepress.org/pages/support or contact us at info@coffeehousepress.org.

JUAN CÁRDENAS (1978) is a Colombian art critic, curator, and author of *Zumbido, Los estratos*, and *Ornamento,* among other titles. He has translated the works of writers such as William Faulkner, Thomas Wolfe, and others. In May 2017, he was named by the Hay Festival in Bogotá as one of the thirty-nine best Latin American writers under the age of thirty-nine. He works as a professor and researcher.

LIZZIE DAVIS is a translator from Spanish to English and an editor at Coffee House Press. Her recent projects include works by Pilar Fraile Amador, Daniela Tarazona, and Elena Medel, and her co-translation of Medel's *Las maravillas* with Thomas Bunstead is forthcoming from Pushkin Press. She has received fellowships from the Omi International Arts Center and the Bread Loaf Translators' Conference in support of her translations.

Ornamental was designed by
Bookmobile Design & Digital Publisher Services.
Text is set in Garamond Premier Pro.